DRAGONWÜLF
BOOK II

Drakwnúlfr

Bók II

TWILIGHT OF THE GODS

Skymning goðanna

A NOVEL BY
SALVATORE DEBELLA

DRAGONWÜLF
BOOK II

Drakwnúlfr

Bók II

TWILIGHT OF THE GODS

Skymning goðanna

A NOVEL BY

SALVATORE DEBELLA

ᛉᚱᚠᚲᛈᛏᚾᛁᛈ — ᛒᛟᚲ II

ᛇᚲᛋᛗᛏᛁᛏᚷ ᚷᛟᛗᚠᛏᛏᚠ

SALVATORE' DEBELLA

DRAGONWÜLF

TWILIGHT OF THE GODS

Old Norse Translations   (poetic / saga style) Translated from the rune carvings discovered by Sir Robert Winterfall in his expeditions of the Underforest (circa 1992-1894).

Rune Carvings done in Elder Futhark Transliterations (approximated) 3rd to 8th Centuries.

DRAGONWÜLF
Book II: Twilight of the Gods
by **Salvatore DeBella**© 2025 Salvatore DeBella
All rights reserved.

ISBN 979-8-90329-412-1

Imprint Staten House

Printed in the United States of America

This book is a work of fiction and not a biography; while real historical figures, events, or public documents may be used, the dialogue, scenes, and interpretations of their personal thoughts or lives are invented for the purpose of the story.
Any resemblance between fictionalized aspects of the real-life person and actual events is coincidental.

This is a work of fiction. Names, characters, places, and incidents are products of the author's imagination or are used fictitiously. Any resemblance to actual persons, living or dead, or actual events is purely coincidental.

WORLD OF DRAGONWÜLF
REALM OF THE HROTHGORN
UNDERFOREST
MORAK THE UNDERSEA
CLIFFS OF ATHGOR
KINGDOM OF THE DRAGONBORNE
KINGDOM OF AROM

Table of contents

Prologue

DR. ALBERT MOREAU LETTER

Dimension of Óðinn 2002 CE

Earth USA

"Historian agit velut musicus peritus, diligenter chordas cuiusque dimensionis tangens"

"He plays history like a skillful musician carefully plucking the strings of each dimension."

My name is Dr. Albert Moreau, and I served as the personal research assistant to Dr. James Winterfall, who compiled the records of *Dragonwülf and the Destiny of Tyr* until he passed away in the 1980s. The record that you are about to read is unusual and sometimes unsettling. I have not altered the text to make it more palatable for a modern audience. It is what it is, and I am simply reporting the findings. My relationship to these records has completely ruined my life. I want nothing more to do with them. I attempted to continue the work begun by Dr. Winterfall's grandfather, Sir Robert Winterfall, in 1894.

Unfortunately, I have been burdened with something that I know is true, but I cannot convince others.

The following record I will present to the reader is a continuation of the records presented by Dr. Winterfall. The manipulation and addition of further records by an unrelenting being in the realms of time demonstrated the urgency to abridge the narrative.

I am aware that a written record that contained the history of a Norse-like civilization that included modern weapons of warfare, Harley-Davidson motorcycles, a pirate ship, and Mafia hitmen seems too implausible to be a reality. I cannot concern myself with what anyone else thinks, and all I desire with all of my heart is to rid myself of this nonsense and to be free of its influence. I wish I had never encountered these records. Nevertheless, I *have* seen them in various forms. I have *read* ancient written descriptions of the things described above, and I have deciphered coded writings that seem to describe machinery or other devices well in advance of the available technology of the time. To a researcher such as me, this is, to say the very least, perplexing.

How can there be ancient records recorded on stone and parchment that tell of the things to come? How can such records exist describing the civilization of other worlds?

I had concluded from my translations that the former Wolfclaw, later known as Dragonwülf, had journeyed far beyond the known realm of existence, crossing into the dimension he referred to as *Höðr*. Höðr (Old Norse: Hǫðr [ˈhɔðz̠] ⓘ, Latin Hotherus; [1] often anglicized as Hod, Hoder, or Hodur) [a] is a god in Norse mythology.

He traversed many treacherous miles above the Earth and the Under-Forest, battling through interdimensional storms and other perils. Finally, he and his crew reached their destination, traveling a great distance in time and space in a Spanish Galleon named *The Deepwater Watchman.*

The ship pursued a renegade to stop him from altering timelines and causing an imbalance in the universe. Many traumatic events in the history of the universe were caused by this being, known also as "sáluflekkir" or The Defiler of Souls. He had discovered a portal that would deliver him to any period in history in the galaxy of his choosing.

Included in this record are the artifacts and journals from the passengers of the Deepwater in their attempt to locate and destroy the Defiler. The passengers of the ship were burdened with the task of reckoning world histories to balance the Universe once again. Each had a personal connection with the Council of beings known as Destiny of Tyr, and each had a reason for altering their own timelines. As you may be familiar with the narrative of *Dragonwülf and the Destiny of Tyr*, the passengers of The Deepwater Watchman were recruited by the council after their individual deaths. Each of the crew was faced with the decision to join the Destiny of Tyr or remain in the clutches of death forever.

The original researcher of these ancient records was Sir Robert Winterfall (1850-1932). He formulated a concept about the universe and co-existing timelines. He called this the Panorama Effect. The effect can be explained by visualizing the universe and timelines as open to view from all directions. The theory states that all timelines can be examined simultaneously in real-time.

Another theory proposed by his grandson, Dr. James Winterfall (1925-1985), is the theory of "The Universal Mirror." This exists only if the process of time is interrupted by an outside force. This causes a time fluctuation or a ripple in time where outside nefarious actors can manipulate outcomes. It remains to be seen if this has validity.

The Many-Worlds Interpretation (Hugh Everett, 1957) suggests that all possible outcomes of every event exist simultaneously, each in its own branching reality.

From that perspective, the universe does not just unfold — it fans out across dimensions, every version happening "at once," but in separate quantum branches.

Einstein and his Block Universe theory says that in relativity, time is treated as a dimension, not as something that "flows," but as something that exists in totality.

I became a firm believer in those theories after the attacks from outside forces seeking to keep these ideas a mystery. This is where The Defiler entered the picture.

I have been visited by a mysterious dark figure during the early morning hours just before dawn on several occasions. This monstrous and ghastly form walked through the walls of my bedchamber and appeared next to my feet at the foot of my bed.

You may believe me to be completely out of my mind, and you might well be correct in assuming that, but I promise I have all of my senses in working order. Let me explain. I believe this was a messenger of The Defiler. I studied his appearances in the ancient texts discovered by Sir Robert Winterfall. I wrote these words as the dark figure spoke them. Given my rudimentary experience with Old Norse, I attempted a rough translation from the spoken word.

"Ek missti fjöllin ór augum mínum. Sólin blindaði mik fyrir öllu undir augnaráði hennar. Vindrinn brenndi andlit mitt ok gerði hár mitt at ösku. Enn lifi ek. Ek mun snúa aptr at heimta þat er mitt er."

Translation from Old Norse.

"I lost the mountains in my eyes. The sun blinded me to all below its gaze. The wind burned my face and turned my hair to ash. Yet I live. I will return to claim what is mine."

I have no explanation, so do not consider that I will give you one. I have no reason to believe that the Defiler lives still, but I believe his followers from Caligulis Q3[1] still do his bidding. Upon further examination of my bedchamber after the departure of the apparition, these runes were burnt into the surface of my oaken writing desk.

ᛗᚲ ᛗᛁᚧᚧᛏᛁ ᚹᛌᛩᚱᚱᛁᛏ ᛩᚱ ᚠᚢᚷᚢᛗ ᛗᛁᛏᚢᛗ

ᚧᛩᚱᛁᛏ ᛒᚱᛁᛏᛗᚠᛗᛁ ᛗᛁᚲ ᚹᛁᚱᛁᚱ ᛩᚱᚱᚢ ᚢᛏᛗᛁᚱ ᚠᚢᚷᛏᚠᚱᚠᛗᛁ ᚺᛗᛏᛏᚠᚱ

ᚹᛁᛏᛗᚱᛁᛏ ᛒᚱᛗᛏᛏᛗᛁ ᚠᛏᛗᚱᛁᛏ ᛗᛁᛏ ᛩᚲ ᚷᛗᚱᛗᛁ ᚺᚠᚱ ᛗᛁᛏ ᚠᛏ ᛩᚧᚲᚢ

ᛗᛏᛏ ᛚᛁᚹᛁ ᛗᚲ

ᛗᚲ ᛗᚢᛏ ᚧᛏᚢᚠ ᚠᚲᛏᚱ ᚠᛏ ᚺᛗᛁᛗᛏᚠ ᚦᚠᛏ ᛗᚱ ᛗᛁᛏᛏ ᛗᚱ

I may be the last in line to receive and study this artifact. I have no assistant, and no researchers are willing to take these theories seriously. I would implore the reader of this record to consider this as a serious subject of study. I feel remorse that I was not able to keep up the work of Sir Robert Winterfall and his grandson, Dr. James Winterfall. If the future is not altered,

I am afraid these stories and histories are destined to remain in the grave with these men, and the Defiler will win his war against humanity.

Can the entirety of all universal events, both past and future, take place simultaneously, appearing in various dimensions at the same time? I believe the answer is yes. In several serious interpretations of physics and philosophy, the entirety of universal events exists simultaneously, merely distributed across dimensions of perception and scale.

We experience only one thread of it at a time, but to the universe itself, everything is eternally and all at once.

I leave you with this question.

Has the Defiler of Souls discovered a way to experience all of these dimensions at once? If so, what is to be done with this knowledge?

Sincerely,
Dr. Albert Moreau
Boston, MA, 2002

Author's Note 2025

On the evening of 20 February 2003, Dr. Albert Moreau was found savagely murdered in his home after what was staged to appear as a home invasion. I believe this was the work of the Defiler of Souls through a corridor of time. My alternative theory is that this is the work of the Defiler's masterpiece, Ogor the Impaler. The Boston Police Department will undoubtedly disagree with me. My connection with Dr. Moreau was not professional, as I am neither an archaeologist nor a researcher of any kind. I am, however, a writer of *somewhat modest* technical skills.

Our connection was through our mutual affiliation with an Edgar Allen Poe readers club. I observed how this manuscript tortured Albert and robbed his life. The original historic record of *Dragonwulf and the Destiny of Tyr* was published in 2022 and written in novel form.

The following record, *The Twilight of the Gods,* was published as a follow-up to *The Destiny of Tyr*.

Dr. Moreau was a brilliant scientist who delved into the mysteries of time and space. He was fascinated by the concept of time travel and spent his entire life researching it. He developed various theories and conducted numerous experiments that brought him closer to his goal of creating a time machine. The contents of his research notes were found scattered around his home and have been compiled into a single record. It appears that Moreau was on the verge of discovering a breakthrough in his time-traveling research when he was tragically killed. One of the most intriguing documents found among his notes was a detailed *blueprint* for a machine he had not yet named. According to his research, the machine or device would be able to transport a passenger through time by activating a series of portals that would briefly open for enough time for a single person to jump through. I believe in my heart that the perpetrator tortured Dr. Moreau to gain more information about his progress on the machine. The brutality of his murder and the desecration of his corpse demonstrated such violent desperation as they attempted to locate the plans for the time machine.

Moreau's research also included a large collection of historical data that he had gathered through various sources. He referred to these sources as artifacts. This data included dates, times, locations, and other pertinent details regarding significant events throughout history. He believed that by using this information, he could travel back in time and witness these events firsthand. Moreau continued the work on the theory about the possibility of multiple timelines coexisting simultaneously. He believed that by traveling back in time and influencing certain events, he could alter the course of history and create a new timeline. Unfortunately, the research was cut tragically short, and his findings have yet to be fully explored. His sudden death was a minor footnote to the archeology and scientific community, but his legacy will continue to inspire those who seek to unravel the mysteries of time. If some unfortunate event befalls me and I end up the victim of foul play, please know it is most likely the work of enemies of time travel. Until we meet again, maybe in the presence of another world.

For your information and curiosity, I present to you *Dr. Albert Moreau's Artifacts.* – Salvatore DeBella

The artifacts are presented as interrelated short tales, vignettes, historical manuscripts, and narratives.

Note: Some creative liberties have been taken for storytelling purposes. The narrative remains intact.

The Pillager of the Silver Cove

Artifact One

PREQUEL

"Hálf-Jón ok ránmenn Silfrviks."

ᚺᚨᛚᚠ-ᛋᛟᛏ ᛟᚲ ᚱᚨᚾᛗᛖᚾᛏ ᛇᛁᛚᚠᚱᚱᛈᛁᚲ

Hálf-Jón and the Pillagers
Of the Silver Cove

Date: Dimension of Óðinn 24 BCE Under-forest Lands

"Hinn mikli 'Úlfakló' mun verða einskis nema hákarls beita, er ek er liðinn með þér!

"The great 'Wolfclaw' will be nothing but shark bait by the time I am through with you!"

Hálf-Jón StoneHeart was known throughout the seas as a courageous but ruthless pirate. He was called Hálf-Jón because in battle, his adversary had attempted to chop him in half from the top of his head with a heavy cutlass. Fortunately, the blade only sank halfway down his forehead, blinding his left eye. His crew described in later years how the sound of his skull against the cutlass haunted even the hardest of men. He only escaped death because of a legendary hard head. He wore the scar like a crown. His ship,

The Pillager of the Silver Cove was a gigantic vessel with ramshackle sails and decayed portholes. The big tub had one foot in the grave, but for reasons that could not be explained, it stayed afloat.

One day, as the crew of the Silver Cove set sail in search of the treasure of the pirate Captain Drekar, Hálf-Jón, with a fiery intensity in his only good eye, thundered orders to his company.

"Secure the mainsail, boys!" he called out, his deep voice floating over the deafening waves. "We are on the hunt for riches, you sons of bitches!" he said, well aware of his rhyme. The Silver Cove, covered in rusted, crumbling steel and bronze fittings over oak planks, stood towering in the waves of the North Sea. It weighed nearly one thousand tons and was nearly one hundred fifty feet in length. When the Silver Cove was built, it required no fewer than two thousand oak trees to complete the frame. It had seen much better days, but the Silver Cove was still as beautiful as when it was launched.

The crew cheered, their spirits lifted by the promise of treasure. The Pillager of the Silver Cove cut through the water like a knife, slicing through the waves with effortless grace. As the crew sailed further into the darkness of the night sea, Hálf-Jón guided his crew toward their prize.

Days turned into weeks as the crew ventured deeper into the waters of the open sea. They faced horrible storms and assorted sea monsters, but Hálf-Jón and his bravery never faltered. He inspired his men with his display of pure guts and stubborn tenacity.

One night, as the crew huddled around the barrel fire on the deck of the ship, Hálf-Jón spun a mostly true, partly false tale from his past. His voice was rich with emotion as he spoke.

"I was born upon the sea, and cut my teeth on the mizzenmast. I grew into manhood, had a family, and when it came time for me to give myself to the sea, I did so like a humble servant of the Queen of the oceans. I sailed the high seas until I returned to port to find out that my wife and children had died in the plague while I was carried away by the sea for so many years. That was the time when my demons hitched a ride on my back. I tried hard to kill the miserable devils, but they just kept on coming for more. I was a husk of a man. I used to have much faith in our God, boys, but after that, I could no longer believe in anything at all. He had abandoned me as if I had walked the plank.

The crew listened, their hearts heavy with the weight of Hálf-Jóns' words. As the fire died down and the night grew cold, a shooting star streaked across the sky. Hálf-Jón saw his opportunity.

"You see that, men?" he said, pointing to the sky. "You never know what comes next. Good or bad, it is all for us to see. What I *can* see is that we are closer than ever to finding the lost treasure of my brother, Captain Drekar. He said that he dumped it on a sandbar while he was being chased by the Royal Navy. He meant to return to pick it up, but his ship and crew were lost in a storm." Hálf-Jón declared, his only eye darting from side to side. "Nothing will stand in our way."

Suddenly, a much larger ship appeared on the horizon, its black flag fluttering in the sea breeze. The Pirate ship, the Bloody Claw, was an impressive sight that cut through the sea. A full-rigged sailing vessel had been stolen from the Navy of the North Sea by Wolfclaw and his crew. They had killed half of the crew of the Navy vessel while the remaining men jumped overboard. *Wolfclaw Thur'Gold*, the notorious pirate known for his ruthlessness and skill in battle, had come to challenge Hálf-Jón for control of the seas. The Bloody Claw came alongside the Silver Cove at her port side. The two Captains came into view of each other.

"Ahoy there, Captain, I have come to claim what is mine! You know well that Drekar's treasure is mine," Wolfclaw's booming voice echoed across the waves, his crew readying their weapons for a surprise ambush.

Hálf-Jón narrowed his eye and gripped his cutlass tightly, a savage grin spreading across his face. "What makes you think the treasure is yours to take?"

"He was my Captain, and I am next in line for his riches," answered Wolfclaw.

"He was my brother, you thief! His gold is mine!" said Hálf-Jón. "He stole it fair and square, and I mean to keep it for my own. You will have to board us and come and get it, ya filthy, sea-scum cutthroat!" said Hálf-Jón, knowing well he did not have the treasure aboard yet.

"I will not have to board your ship, you bottom dweller! I will ram The Bloody Claw down your throat!" answered Captain Wolfclaw, his voice carried over the water expanse between the two ships. "Now lower your cannons!"

"That is the only way you will ever board the Silver Cove, you coward!" shouted Hálf-Jón.

"Hard turn port side, first mate," Captain Wolfclaw ordered. "Ram her hard!"

With a deafening roar, the two ships collided, and the planks were fixed to the Pillager. Wolfclaw and the crew of the Bloody Claw boarded The Silver

Cove. A clash of metal rang out as the pirates were entangled in a bloody battle. Wolfclaw, his tall and imposing figure covered in scars, wielded a wickedly sharp cutlass with ease. A wolf's claw was still buried in his face after he fought a she-wolf with his bare hands. Wolfclaw left it there as a warning to his enemies. Hálf-Jón, a nimble and agile fighter, moved around his opponent, his twin daggers flashing in the chaos of battle.

"You should never have come to my *part* of the sea, Hálf-Jón! I will make damn sure your bones come to rest at the bottom of Davy Jones' locker!" Wolfclaw snarled, his eyes filled with anger.

Hálf-Jón laughed heartily, his green eyes and red beard almost glowing in the night. "I have faced worse than the likes of you! The great 'Wolfclaw' will be nothing but shark bait by the time I am through with you! Your half-eaten corpse will remain in your *part* of the sea- the bilgy bottom muck."

The clash of steel continued, pirates, matching the other blow for blow, their skill and determination on display for all to see. The deck ran slick with blood as the fight raged on, neither pirate crew willing to back down in the face of death.

Hálf-Jón saw his opening. With a swift and calculated strike, he disarmed Wolfclaw, sending his cutlass clattering to the deck below.

"You may be ruthless, Wolfclaw, but you lack the heart of a true pirate!" Hálf-Jón declared, his voice ringing out over the sound of the waves.

Defeated and bloodied, Wolfclaw Thur'Gold sank to his knees and touched the wolf's claw in his face one final time before he bowed his head in submission. "Finish it, then, Hálf-Jón. Send me to the depths and claim your victory."

However, Hálf-Jón, ever the honorable pirate, extended a hand to his fallen foe. "We may be enemies on the high seas, Wolfclaw, but we are both pirates. Your life is yours to keep this day. But remember this: should our paths cross again, I will kill you."

Wolfclaw turned and limped back to his ship, left to ponder the mercy of his sworn enemy.

THE NORTH HUNDREN

Many years on, Hálf-Jón and Wolfclaw Thur'Gold found themselves much older, as new crewmates on the deck of the North Hundren, their eyes locked in a fierce glare as they faced each other once again. Hálf-Jón, with his weathered face and rugged beard, had come to be known across the seas as a cunning pirate with a heart as black as the night. Wolfclaw Thur'Gold was a ruthless cutthroat with a reputation for leaving a trail of destruction in his wake.

Hálf-Jón narrowed his only eye to Wolfclaw Thur'Gold. "I do not take kindly to sharing a ship with the likes of *him*, Captain," he growled, his hand hovering over the hilt of his saber. I told the piece of sea trash many years ago that I would kill him if I saw him. I did, and I am going to!"

The Captain of the North, Hundren, Old-Turas, a grizzled old seafarer, stood between them, his hands raised in a gesture of peace. "Alright, boys," he said, his voice carrying over the sound of the crashing waves. "I will not have any killin' on my ship. We have a long voyage ahead of us, and there is no room for bloodshed unless I am the one lettin' the blood."

Wolfclaw Thur'Gold sneered, his hand resting on the cutlass at his side. "And I do not fancy being stuck in this *tub* with *him* either," he retorted.

"The Hundren *is not* a tub! "Old-Turas sighed, rubbing his temples wearily. He had heard tales of the fierce rivalry between Hálf-Jón and Wolfclaw Thur'Gold, and he knew that their tempers could spark a mutiny if left unchecked. "Listen here, you two miserable old fools," he said. "I will not have trouble on my ship. If you cannot settle this now, then I will throw both of your arses off the ship."

Hálf-Jón and Wolfclaw Thur'Gold exchanged a wary glance, neither willing to back down from the challenge. After a tense moment of silence, Hálf-Jón spoke, his voice low but steady. "Fine, we will settle this like pirates," he said, gesturing to the open deck. I have to keep my word.

"That is what worries me," said Wolfclaw. I cannot just stand by and wait for you to kill me." Wolfclaw Thur'Gold grinned with anticipation. "Stand fast and gird up your loins, Hálf-Jón! Make peace with Róthul-Orkr, the whale god, and prepare to die!”

As Captain Old-Turas and the rest of the crew watched on, the clash of steel rang out across the deck as the two pirates fought.

“I am not afraid of your blade, Hálf-Jón. Bring it to me and let me quench my thirst!” Wolfclaw taunted as he raised his cutlass to his lips and licked the blade.

“I think you are mad!” Hálf-Jón said, his face set in bewilderment. “Not *everyone* on the sea fears you. They just think you are an old fool, a drinker of mead, an old drunk.”

“Who does not fear me? Who said these things? Bring him here and let him tell me to my face!” answered Wolfclaw to the taunt of Hálf-Jón.

“Oh, I have your attention now! Your reputation is not what you think!”

The duel raged on, each pirate matching the other blow for blow. Blood mingled with the salt of the sea air as they circled each other, their eyes locked in a fierce battle of wills. As drops of blood became streams and the sun began to fall, it became clear that neither of the pirates would beat the other. Time came to a dragging crawl.

“I cannot lose much more blood,” said an exhausted Wolfclaw. “My wounds run freely and must be bound. I cannot go on.”

“How many times do I have to beat your worthless arse in one lifetime?” taunted Hálf-Jón.

"It is done. If you concede that you cannot fight on, then I will lower my weapon," said Hálf-Jón.

"Only if you lower yours first," said Wolfclaw.

"Do not force my hand, you fool!" said Half-John.

The two pirates locked eyes in an icy stare, their weapons lowered in weary acknowledgment of each other's skill. It was a draw. A rare and unexpected outcome that left the crew of the North Hundren stunned into silence.

Captain Old-Turas grinned, clapping his hands together in approval. "Well, I'll be damned," he exclaimed. "It looks like we have got ourselves a pair of unlikely shipmates after all. Work together for the good of the ship, or *I will kill* both of you and strip you of your worthless pelts."

ARTIFACT TWO

KJALAR-DRÁTTUR

THE KEELHAUL

Keelhaul punishment by dragging a sailor through the water under the keel of a ship. Author translation from Old Norse

DATE: DIMENSION OF ÓÐINN 140 CE UNDER FOREST LANDS, THIRD KING TIN'OLD, SON OF THE LOST PRINCE

Many more years have passed into the next centuries in the vast waters of the North Sea. The North Hundren sailed proudly, its crew of ruthless pirates led by the now first mate Wolfclaw. Hálf-Jón had departed and regained his position as Captain of the Pillager of the Silver Cove. The North Hundren had seen many battles and raids, its reputation striking fear into the hearts of sailors everywhere.

Captain Santiago Old-Turas was still the Captain of the North Hundren. His victories were legendary, but dissent soon grew among the crew. Many of the men felt Old-Turas was only looking out for his own riches and not sharing the spoils with the crew. Whispers of discontent spread at a furious pace.

One fateful night, under the cloak of darkness and by the light of the moon, Wolfclaw gathered a group of disgruntled men in the belly of the ship.

"We have had enough of Old-Turas's greed. It is time for a change to make things more even," Wolfclaw growled, his eyes blazing with excitement. "He has led us to countless battles, but what have we recovered? We must have a Captain who values our coin purses as much as his own. Most of all, we need another Captain who will show our worth with more gold."

"Who might that new Captain be?" asked a crewmember.

"All of you know that I can do it and be fair to all of you," answered Wolfclaw.

"That is what we thought!" said the crewmember. "You cannot be trusted with anything, you are a terrible fighter, and you are filthier than the rest of us ever thought of being. I say nay!"

The men whispered amongst each other, their voices hushed but filled with a profound sense of rebellion.

"I say it should be Captain Wolfclaw!" said another crewmember.

"I accept the challenge! If any among you wish to usurp me, you will feel my steel!" boasted Wolfclaw.

The remaining men murmured their agreement, so, as the night wore on, they created a plan to ensure that their mutiny would be swift and effective.

The next morning, as the sun rose over the horizon, chaos erupted on board The North Hundren. Wolfclaw and his followers sprang into action, confronting Captain Old-Turas on the deck of the ship.

"Captain, your presence is requested," Wolfclaw declared.

"Who needs me below?"

"There is a fight over a dice game in the galley, and it has spilled over into the men's quarters," said Wolfclaw.

"We will see about this! There will be none of this aboard the North Hundren!" bellowed Old-Turas. Just then, out of the corner of his eye, he spotted a loyal crewmember looking around the yardarm slowly but convincingly *nodding his head no…* in warning.

"Do you think I am a fool? Look at me, Wolfclaw! Do you think I am a fool? Did you think you could get me below and ambush me?" said Turas incredulously. "I am too old and have seen too much to fall for such a poorly thought-out plan.

"Turn the ship over to me. The crew stands with me. Will you forfeit the wheel?" asked Wolfclaw.

Captain Old-Turas's eyes widened in disbelief, and his hand instinctively reached for his own weapon. "You dare to mutiny me, Wolfclaw? I took you in when you were, but a mere vagabond, and this is how you repay me?"

The mutineers sprang into action, swinging cutlasses and daggers at the Captain and his loyalists.

The ring of steel was heard across the ship as the mutiny unfolded; the deck was already slick with the blood of fallen mutineers. Men fought with a ferocity born of desperation, each side determined to emerge victorious in this deadly power struggle until most of the traitors' bodies lay twisted in bloody death.

Amidst the chaos, Wolfclaw and Captain Old-Turas engaged in a fierce duel, their swords dancing in a deadly ballet of skill and rage. The crew watched in tense silence, their loyalties torn between the old captain and the daring usurper.

Finally, with a swift and calculated strike, Captain Old-Turas disarmed Wolfclaw, the tip of his blade pressing against his throat.

"Have you ever won a sword fight in your entire life?" taunted Old-Turas. "I think this might be a bad choice for your life's work. Perhaps you would make a better galley cook."

The defeated pirate's eyes burned with a mix of anger and resignation.

"Finish it, then," Wolfclaw rasped, his voice heavy with defeat.

The Captain's grip on his sword wavered, a flicker of doubt crossing his face. "No, there is no sport in just killing you on the deck. You are no longer fit to be a pirate in my crew. I will spare your life, but you will pay dearly for what you have done. When I am finished, you will wish for the sweet release of death.”

With a scream of defeat, Wolfclaw cast aside his weapon, signaling the end of the mutiny. The crew watched in tense silence as Old-Turas’ men captured the Norse warrior and tied him to the main mast.

“Want us to gut ‘im like a tuna, Cap'n?” asked one of the pirates.

“Yeah, we could just slit his throat and let him bleed out, we could!” said another pirate.

The Captain thought for a moment and decided on Wolfclaw’s fate.

“Prepare the ship, grab some ropes. We are going to keelhaul this old fool.”

A sense of trepidation pervaded the crew as the captain ordered the keelhauling of Wolfclaw. Somehow, being gutted like a tuna seemed a more humane punishment than keelhauling. The sun glared fiercely overhead as the crew gathered around the deck, their faces reflecting a mixture of fear and anticipation. Wolfclaw stood stoic and unyielding, his eyes fixed on the churning water below.

“You will pay for your treachery, Wolfclaw,” bellowed Captain Old-Turas, his grizzled face contorted in a mixture of anger and satisfaction. “Prepare yourself, the depths await you.”

The crewmembers, their faces hidden beneath shadowy bandanas, whispered among themselves, their voices hushed as they watched the scene unfold. The sailors began to tie thick ropes around Wolfclaw's wrists and ankles, securing him tightly.

Wolfclaw's eyes never wavered, his gaze piercing through the veil of impending doom. "I will meet my fate with my head held high," he declared, his voice steady and unwavering.

"Aye, you do just that and say 'good day' to Davy Jones while you are under there for us, will ya?" said the Captain.

As the crew hoisted Wolfclaw over the side of the ship, the sound of the waves crashing against the wooden hull filled the air. The water below churned ferociously, eager to claim its next victim. The crewmembers began to lower Wolfclaw into the frothy depths, the ropes creaking under the strain.

"May Róthul-Orkr ^(The Whale Deity) have mercy on yer soul," muttered a grizzled old sailor, his voice barely audible above the roar of the sea.

Suddenly, with a deafening splash, Wolfclaw was plunged into the icy waters below. The crew watched in tense silence as the ropes dragged him beneath the ship, his body scraping against the barnacled hull. The sound of his agonized screams arose from the sea, sending shivers down the spines of even the hardiest sailors. The fact that they could hear underwater screams was terrifying for the men.

Minutes passed like hours as Wolfclaw was dragged along the width of the ship, his body battered and broken by the merciless keelhauling. Just when it seemed that he could not have possibly survived, the crew began to pull him back on board, his bloodied form limp and unconscious.

As Wolfclaw lay gasping for breath on the deck, Captain Old-Turas stood over him, a cruel smirk playing on his lips. "You are lucky to be alive, you scoundrel," he sneered. "But remember this day, for the *sea* never forgets. Put him in a dinghy and maroon him! I never want to see his hairy carcass again!" the captain ordered.

As the ship sailed on, the ghosts of the fallen men whispered on the wind, their sacrifice forever etched into the annals of maritime lore. The Captain and his crew set sail while pirate Wolfclaw floated marooned on the sea.

Some months later, Captain Old-Turas discovered that Wolfclaw had been picked up by some anglers and brought to the coastal town of Watershire at the edge of the Kingdom of Arom.

"This will not do!" said the angry Captain. "Wolfclaw was meant to be lost at sea, not enjoying a holiday at some seaport."

After eluding the Captain's search many years later, Wolfclaw Thur'Gold returned to his people in the Underforest, gave up pirating, and created an army of Aromites to defeat the evil King of the Hrothgorn. Wolfclaw also sought out the help of an unlikely ally, old enemy Captain Old-Turas and his crew, to defeat King Draknorr and his Hrothgorn army.

As fate would have it, after victory in the Arom Hrothgorn war, Wolfclaw was murdered by one of his own men. As he was being carried to Valhalla, he was interrupted by The Destiny of Tyr, who resurrected his body and gave him a new name, *'Dragonwülf.'*

These are the tales of Dragonwülf and the Twilight of the Gods.

Artifact Three

VARÐRIR Í SKUGGUM

THE WATCHERS IN THE SHADOWS

DATE: FUTURE DIMENSION OF HÖÐR (2296 CE)

"We were dead and refused to lie down in our graves, and that is why we will succeed where others have failed."

-Dragonwülf

The outer-space galleon *The Deepwater Watchman* floated silently through the dark space of the Eastern galaxy, its sails billowing in the cold outer darkness as the crew went about their nightly duties. Captain Old-Turas was at the wheel of his new ship, his eyes scanning deep space for any signs of danger. Suddenly, a shimmering portal appeared on the deck, and out stepped the council of mysterious beings known as The Destiny of Tyr.

"Every time you creepy beasties do that, it gives me the willies!" said Old-Turas. "At least ya' could give me a heads up next time."

Their presence sent a shiver down the spines of the crew.

The leader of The Destiny was Avat'or, a figure cloaked in shadows with eyes that seemed to glow with an otherworldly light. He stepped forward and spoke in a voice that echoed like distant thunder. "Captain Old-Turas and Dragonwülf, we have come to deliver a message of great importance. The fate of the entire realm hangs in the balance."

"Good!" said Dragonwülf. We are prepared for what is to come. We have agreed to return to life to serve you. What are we to do?"

"In time, we will reveal this to you," said Avat'or. "In the meantime, you will travel to gather your gallery of rogues that have been chosen for you to complete your missions."

"Missions?" Dragonwülf growled low in his throat. "Speak plainly; we have no time for riddles anymore."

Avat'or's eyes gleamed as they regarded Dragonwülf. "There is a darkness rising in the galaxy, a force of unimaginable power that threatens to consume everything in its path. Only by uniting the realms of men can this evil be vanquished."

Captain Old-Turas nodded solemnly, his mind racing with the enormity of the task set before them.

"We will do whatever it takes to protect our world from this threat. We have much history together. The Destiny of Tyr saved the army of Arom at the Battle of the Cliffs of Athgor."

As the council members took their seats on the ship's deck, an imposing figure known as Stjarna (Star) stepped forward.

"Stjarna speaks for the Destiny of Tyr on this day. Hear her!" said Avat'or.

Her voice was a gentle whisper, yet carried the weight of centuries as she began to speak, her words reverberating through the clearing.

"We are the Destiny of Tyr," Stjarna announced, her eyes glowing with light. "We are the guardians of this world, tasked with preserving the balance and protecting it from those who seek to do it harm."

One by one, the council members begin to share their stories, their voices a blend of glory and power.

"It was in the age of men when the kingdoms were involved in an awful power struggle," Stjarna began. "One kingdom, ruled by a vicious and tyrannical king named Malakar, tried to conquer all others and bend them to his will. We could not stand by as his armies destroyed the lands of the innocent," she continued. "We descended from our celestial homes to find one who could rescue the innocents."

The crew listened intently as the elder described how they had appeared before a young warrior named Wolfclaw, who had been chosen to be the one to overthrow Malakar's cruelty. He was chosen for his heart and his belief in justice. As he had not been an exceptional warrior, they had imbued him with strength and courage, guiding his hand in battle and whispering words of wisdom in his ear.

"That was the Destiny of Tyr?" asked a shocked Dragonwülf, the former Wolfclaw. "Malakar was destroyed by my hand, not by you!"

"Without our guiding hand and words of wisdom, it may not have been so," said Avat'or.

"So it was," continued Stjarna, that Wolfclaw rallied the people of the realm to this cause."

As the echoes of their tale lingered in the minds of the listeners, they knew that the Destiny of Tyr was a force not to be trifled with, a guiding hand in the vast tapestry of the universe.

"We have watched over this world since the dawn of time," said another member of the Destiny with the form of a majestic eagle, its wings unfurled in a dramatic display. "We have seen civilizations rise and fall, and through it all, we have remained in our duty."

A being with the appearance of a Norseman added, "It is not our place to interfere directly in the affairs of mortals, but we lend our guidance in subtle ways, nudging them towards paths that lead to ultimate victory."

"We are the keepers of the balance, the watchers in the shadows," Stjarna declared, her voice resonating with a quiet power. "As long as the Council of Tyr exists, we shall be here, guiding its *destiny* and ensuring that it lives forever."

With a final nod from Avat'or, the council members dispersed, and their forms faded into space as they returned to their unseen duties. Only Avat'or remained on the Deepwater.

Former mortal enemies Captain Old Turas and Dragonwülf had been through many battles together, their bond forged in the fires of war. Now, they faced their most daunting challenge yet - a mission that could change the fate of the entire world.

"Dragonwülf, my old friend," Captain Turas began, his voice grave and filled with purpose. "The council has called upon us to undertake a mission of great importance. They speak of a darkness that threatens to consume our land, a darkness that only we can hope to defeat."

Dragonwülf nodded solemnly. "I am ready, old man. What I really wanted to do was to continue my journey to Valhalla, but I died at the hand of one of my own men just to be brought back by Destiny for this. He was a Filthy assassin. I hope it was worth it. A cross bolt to the neck is very painful."

Captain Turas's gaze turned steely. "You know that we are not like other men. We have faced death countless times and lived to tell the tale. We were both dead and refused to lie down in our graves, and that is why we will succeed where others have failed. The Destiny of Tyr has been with you always, it seems, and you did not even know it. You, my friend, are more important than I once thought," said Old-Turas. "More than anyone knows, it seems."

"That is enough tales of my exploits for one day," said Dragonwülf.

"I witnessed Wolfclaw in the defeat of Malakar. I would be glad to tell you what this brave old pirate did," said Avat'or.

"Please spare us. I can bear to hear no more stories about this today," pleaded Dragonwülf.

"I must speak of this brave one, your Captain and friend must hear of your bravery. King Malakar sent the people into terror and stole from the land. He spread hate and fear throughout the Kingdom. The people lived in constant fear, their spirits crushed under the weight of his cruel rule," he explained. One day, Wolfclaw came at the behest of the Destiny of Tyr. The people had heard of a fierce warrior who roamed the kingdom's forests, striking fear into the hearts of those who were in the court of the king. His identity was secret, and his motives were unknown to all, but I knew him from his birth. As the people whispered of rebellion, King Malakar grew paranoid, sending his enforcers to find and kill any threats to his rule. The kingdom was on the brink of collapse.

One night, as the full moon cast a glow over the land, Wolfclaw emerged from the shadows, his heart in flames with determination. He made his way to the castle, his footsteps silent as he crept through the deserted corridors, evading the king's guards with skill.

At the heart of the castle, King Malakar sat on his throne, his expression twisted as he gazed out over his kingdom. He sensed a presence in the room and spun around, his eyes widening in shock as he beheld the figure of Wolfclaw standing before him.

'Guards attend to me,' the king thundered, his voice echoing through the chamber.

'I am Wolfclaw, I am of no consequence and no special skill,' he replied, his voice cold and hard as steel. "*I am nobody*. When they ask who killed you today, your people will reply, nobody killed him."

"Wolfclaw drew his broadsword and demanded," On your feet or on your knees! Your choice."

A fierce battle ensued, the clash of swords ringing through the halls as Wolfclaw and King Malakar fought with all their might. The King proved a capable foe, but Wolfclaw's skill and determination were unmatched. With each strike, he chipped away at the king's defenses, drawing closer to victory with every passing moment.

Finally, with a mighty roar, Wolfclaw delivered the final blow, his sword piercing the heart of the evil king. King Malakar uttered a scream of rage and despair as he crumpled to the ground, fading away like shadows in the light of dawn.

As the kingdom rejoiced, Wolfclaw's identity was revealed to all. Now we know that he is Dragonwülf, a legendary warrior blessed with the blood of dragons, who had come to free the kingdom from the grip of darkness," said Avat'or as he finished his tale.

"I think you build me up too much. Indeed, I do not deserve that," said Dragonwülf.

"You have the blood of Dragons coursing through you!" said Avat'or.

"I no more have the blood of dragons than you. It was Avat'or and the Destiny of Tyr who had shown me mercy and given me back my life. I can ask no more from you. Today, I journey with you on our ship as equal men in search of the same thing. You owe me nothing except your honor, bravery, and the might to do what is to be done," said Dragonwülf. "You have it and much more. I am at your service."

Artifact Four

THE WORDS OF ÓÐINN

orð Óðins

ᚩᚱᛞ ᚩᚦᛁᛏᚲ

DIMENSION OF ÓÐINN 127 BCE
UNDER-FOREST LANDS

The Palace Of Stone

"Vér verðum at faðma hið ókenda með hugrekki ok slægð. Minniz, börn mín, at jafnvel í myrkvum tímum er ætíð örlítið bjarma ljóss. Svá er með von." — Óðinn

ᚠᛗᚱ ᚠᛗᚱᛗᚢᛗ ᚠᛏ ᚤᚠᛞᛗᚠ ᚻᛁᛗ ᚩᚲᛗᛏᛗᚠ

ᛗᛖᚦ ᚺᚢᚷᚱᛖᚲᚲᛁ ᛟᚲ ᛊᛚᚨᚷᚦ

ᛗᛁᚾᚾᛁᛉ ᛒᛟᚱᚾ ᛗᛁᚾ

ᚨᛏ ᛃᚨᚡᚾᚹᛖᛚ ᛁ ᛗᛃᚱᚲᚹᚢᛗ ᛏᛁᛗᚢᛗ

ᛖᚱ ᚨᛏᛁᛞ ᚨᚢᚱᛚᛁᛏᛁᛚ ᛒᛃᚨᚱᛗᚨ ᛚᛃᛟᛊᛊ

ᛊᚹᚨ ᛖᚱ ᛗᛖᚦ ᚹᛟᚾ

— ᛟᛞᛁᚾ

We must embrace the unknown with courage and cunning. Remember, my children, even in the darkest of times, there is always a tiny flicker of light. So it is with hope."

-Óðinn

In the Palace of Stone in the ancient city of Arom, Óðinn stood on the steps, his one eye gleaming with wisdom and power. Queen Valkyrja stepped down from her throne to allow a higher elevation for Óðinn to speak. A hush fell over the crowd as they gathered to hear his words.

"Dear mortals of Arom and beyond," Óðinn's voice boomed, echoing through the cobblestone streets. "I appear before you in spirit as well as to the brave souls of Asgard today to deliver a grave warning. Darkness looms on the horizon, a threat unlike any we have ever faced."

Gasps rippled through the crowd as Óðinn's words sank in. Queen Valkyrja stepped forward, her eyes wide with admiration and awe. "What do you mean, All-Father? What darkness threatens us?"

Óðinn fixed the Queen with a steely gaze. "A lost god known as *The Defiler of Souls* has awakened from his slumber. He seeks to bring chaos and destruction upon the realms. His thirst for power knows no bounds, and his cruelty knows no mercy."

Whispers erupted among the crowd, fear and uncertainty written on their faces. A grizzled warrior named Svæin stepped forward, his voice strong despite the tremor in his hands. "What can we do, All-Father? How can we hope to defeat him?"

Óðinn smiled, a rare expression of warmth on his weathered face. "I will stand by your side, my children. I will fight alongside you and lend you my strength. Nevertheless, remember, the true power lies within each of you. Believe in yourselves, believe in each other, and together we can overcome any obstacle, no matter how insurmountable it may seem. I have summoned a warrior from among you."

"Who is this warrior, All-Father?" asked the Queen. "Will we see him soon?"

"You will know of his arrival soon," said Óðinn. "I have arranged his entry through the Destiny of Tyr."

"The Destiny is well known to me as they helped to defeat the evil King Draknorr," said the Queen.

"Very good, then our Queen of Arom awaits the arrival of one known as Dragonwülf," said Óðinn.

"He is not known to me," said the Queen.

"Receive him with thankfulness. You will know him when you see him," proclaimed Óðinn.

"Yes, we look forward to his arrival," said the Queen. "You have brought great honor to our kingdom, Father Óðinn," Queen Valkyrja said, her eyes reflecting pride and gratitude. "Your courage and strength have kept our lands safe, and for that, we are eternally grateful."

Óðinn added a warning," Do not take the power of The Defiler lightly and do not take his defeat as a foregone conclusion. Until I return, take care of one another and fight with all that is in you."

The crowd erupted into cheers, their voices raised in a chorus of hope and determination. Óðinn watched with pride the brave souls who had gathered before him. As the sun dipped below the horizon, the people of Arom and their brave Queen stood together in their fight against the darkness that threatened to consume them all.

So begins the age of Dragonwülf and the Destiny of Tyr.

The Ice Giants and the Enceladus Moon Colony

In the distant reaches of the solar system, on the surface of Saturn's moon Enceladus, a peaceful colony thrived under a peaceful leadership council. The colony flourished with a harmonious coexistence with those around them. One day in the dimension of Thor in the year 2396 CE, everything changed as a band of ice giants, exiled by their own kind, descended upon the moon.

In the icy expanse of the universe, the ice giants roamed. These towering and menacing creatures had long been exiled from their homeland for their rebellious ways and thirst for power beyond measure. They thirsted for revenge against those who exiled them.

As they journeyed through the cosmos, the ice giants stumbled upon the serene moon. Their eyes flashed with unholy revenge as they beheld the unspoiled beauty that lay before them. With a deafening roar that echoed through the emptiness of space, they descended upon the moon, their massive forms overcoming the frozen landscape.

One by one, the giant ice monsters unleashed their frozen powers, sending forth a powerful wave of hard ice that enveloped the moon in a blanket of freezing despair. The gentle whispers of the breezes were replaced by the howling of a never-ending blizzard wind.

The unaware inhabitants of Enceladus were filled with sorrow and disbelief as they gazed upon the devastation brought down by the ice giants.

"We have no mercy for you and your people. We were given none, and you will receive none! We are the forgotten ones, the outcasts of our kind," boomed the leader of the ice giants, his voice as cold and unyielding as the frozen mountains. "We have come to claim this moon as our own, to reign supreme."

The Queen of Enceladus trembled with fear and defiance, her radiant form flickering in the harsh light of the ice giants. "You may have frozen this land, but you will never extinguish the light that shines within each living being," she declared, her voice ringing out with unyielding resolve.

In one swoop of his icy hand, one of the ice giants covered the Queen with a thick layer of death ice and enclosed the Queen in eternal death sleep.

"Sleep well, Your Majesty, in your royal slumber with the Kings and Queens of the ages," said an ice giant.

During the eternal ice age that now gripped the moon, a spark of hope ignited within the hearts of its inhabitants. The creatures of the moon banded together to resist the tyranny of the renegade ice giants. With courage and ingenuity, they launched a daring campaign to reclaim their home and restore balance to the once-peaceful world.

The battle raged on for ages, the clash of ice and light echoing across the frozen landscape. Through hardships and sacrifice, the moon inhabitants stood united against the oppressive rule of the ice giants.

In the end, it was the might of the ice giants that prevailed, despite the unwavering courage and unity of those who called the moon their home. As the echoes of the battle faded into the cosmic winds, a new chapter began for the moon, a chapter filled with death, despair, and the triumph of darkness over light.

The giant ice creatures, towering and menacing, unleashed a powerful wave of frost that enveloped the moon, plunging it into an eternal ice age. The colony's once-vibrant landscape now lay frozen and desolate, its inhabitants struggling to survive against the onslaught of the ruthless renegades.

Amidst the chaos, a group of survivors emerged, twisted by the cruelty of the ice giants and the harsh conditions of their new world. They banded together, forming a cult-like society centered on a grand temple of ice. High priests arose from their ranks, wielding dark powers fueled by their desire for power and control.

"Bow before our powers and worship the gods that we create for you! We will take you under our wings and guide you into the right thinking! Trust us with your care."

Within the temple's walls, eerie chants echoed through the icy corridors, and rituals were conducted to harness the frigid energy of the moon itself. The high priests, draped in frost-covered robes, held sway over their followers with promises of salvation through the mastery of the magical ice arts.

The Rise of the Holy Temple

In the aftermath of the brutal Ice Giant Wars on the icy moon of Enceladus, some of the survivors banded together to form a temple to govern and rule over the weaker remnants of their kind. The temple stood tall and formidable amidst the frozen landscape, a symbol of power and authority in the desolate land.

Among the leaders of the temple were Xemius, High Priest of Ice, a formidable figure known for his icy demeanor and unwavering devotion to the ancient ways, and Jarvis Nightwish, the enigmatic High Executioner with a reputation for ruthless efficiency and unwavering loyalty. It had become necessary to appoint a high executioner as a method of controlling the people of the temple and to maintain the sacred rituals of the temple. Any member caught speaking ill of the temple would feel the wrath of Jarvis Nightwish and the *Disruptor*.

One frosty morning, as the wind howled through the icy corridors of the temple, the High Priest of Ice summoned Jarvis Nightwish to his chambers. "Jarvis, we face a new threat," the High Priest intoned, his voice as cold as the ice that surrounded them. "There are murmurs of dissent among the survivors. They grow restless, questioning our authority and challenging our rule."

Jarvis Nightwish nodded, his steely eyes gleaming in the dim light of the chamber. "I will see to it, High Priest," he replied, his voice low and commanding. "Those who dare to defy us will face the full extent of my disruptor."

As the days passed, tensions mounted within the temple walls. Whispers of rebellion spread like wildfire, threatening to tear apart the fragile peace that had been established in the wake of the war.

One fateful night, a group of dissidents rose up against the temple leaders, their voices raised in defiance, as they sought to challenge the authority that had been imposed upon them. The High Priest of Ice and Jarvis Nightwish sprang into action; his tongue was sharp and decisive as he faced off against the rebels.

"You dare to defy us?" The High Priest thundered, his voice ringing out through the icy corridors. "You will pay dearly for your treachery!" he screamed into the face of the leader of the rebels.

Jarvis Nightwish stepped forward, his disruptor gleaming in the faint light of the chamber. "I warned you," he growled, his eyes blazing with a fierce determination. "Now, face the consequences of your actions."

In a swift and brutal display of power, Jarvis Nightwish unleashed his wrath upon the rebels. The tip of the Disruptor sliced through the icy air and aimed with deadly precision. The High Priest of Ice stood by his side, his words echoing with a chilling finality as he pronounced judgment upon the leader of the rebellion who dared to challenge their authority.

"Member of the temple, citizen P38, stand at attention! You have been found guilty of blasphemy against the Temple of the People. You will feel the wrath of the disruptor," said the High Priest. The Disruptor ray touched member P38 and dissolved her into a shrieking, fading pile of instant ashes.

As the final echoes of the shrieks of P38 faded into the icy night, the survivors of the Ice Giant Wars bowed their heads in submission, their rebellious spirits quelled by the unyielding force of the temple leaders. The High Priest of Ice and Jarvis Nightwish stood victorious, their rule unchallenged as they gazed out over the frozen landscape, their dialogue echoing through the icy winds as a warning to all who would dare to defy them.

ARTIFACT FIVE

DRAUMAR DRAKÚLFS

Dragonwülf's Dreams

Date: Dimension of Óðinn 124 CE

"Ek finna hugg. Í bergmáli kvǫl minnar, ek finna styrk. Í eldi hefnda minnar, ek finna tilgang." –Dragonwülf

"I find solace. In the echoes of my pain, I find strength. In the fire of my revenge, I find purpose."

The events of Dragonwülf and the Destiny of Tyr have taken place and cemented themselves into the crowded streets of time. The war against the evil King Draknorr and his warriors, the Hrothgorn, has finished its course. King Draknorr was killed by the Queen's sword, and his palace of Bones was burnt to the ground. Dragonwülf fully expected to be carried to Valhalla as promised, but it was not meant to be. He was resurrected from the bottom of the sea and forced to serve the Destiny of Tyr in return. Queen Valorii returned to her Kingdom.

The old warrior fell asleep in the corner of the Great Hall of the Ancients as he awaited an audience with Avat'or, the leader of The Destiny of Tyr. The sheer warmth and quiet of the hall caused him to drift into a dream. He floated into a vapor that surrounded his head with visions of days yet to be and deeds that were still but an illusion. Suddenly, in spirit, he was on a familiar ship. The tide lapped the sides as the sea mist fell upon his face like a baptism of adventure and fire.

He was lost in thought and vision.

What I dream comes from the pain I hold. Heavy is the sword that rests upon my back. It gave me life, and now its weight seeks to kill me. I can hear the echoes of the mighty ice giants in the forest and on the face of the sea. These ghostly voices are yet to come, but I know I will hear them. Their roars and shrieks will never die!

In Dragonwülf's dream, in the heart of the Scandinavian wilderness, a village stood in peril. A fierce demon giant known as Drol'gar had descended upon the peaceful settlement, unleashing chaos and destruction upon its inhabitants. The villagers trembled in fear as they watched their homes burn, and their loved ones fall.

Amidst the chaos, Dragonwülf emerged from the shadows. Clad in armor adorned with intricate symbols and wielding a mighty sword forged in the fires of the gods. He surveyed the scene before him, his steely gaze fixed upon the towering demon giant. With a resolute determination burning in his eyes, he raised his sword high and shouted, "I am Dragonwülf, defender of the innocent and scourge of the wicked. By the blood of my ancestors, I shall vanquish the foul beast and raise his bloody head on a pike!"

Drol'gar turned his malevolent gaze upon Dragonwülf, a cruel grin spreading across his twisted features. "Come forth and meet your death!" the demon giant boomed, his voice echoing like thunder. "You are a helpless worm before my might. Remain, and I will kill you quickly. If I must seek you, your death will be slow and painful!"

Undeterred, Dragonwülf charged towards the demon giant, his sword gleaming in the light of the burning village. The two adversaries clashed in a titanic struggle, their blows shaking the very earth beneath them. With each strike, Dragonwülf's sword glowed brighter with the power of the gods, while Drol'gar's dark magic crackled around him like a malevolent storm.

As the battle raged on, the villagers watched in awe and terror, their hearts filled with hope as they saw their champion waging war against the forces of darkness. They whispered prayers to the Norse gods, beseeching them to grant Dragonwülf the strength to overcome the demon giant and save their village from certain destruction.

Finally, with a mighty roar that shook the heavens, Dragonwülf delivered a decisive blow that struck deep into the Demon giant's black heart. The giant howled in agony, his form dissolving into a swirling vortex of darkness before vanishing entirely.

The village fell silent as Dragonwülf stood victorious amidst the ruins, his chest heaving with exertion and his sword dripping with the blood of his fallen foe. The villagers rushed forward and hailed him as their savior and protector.

Dragonwülf simply nodded, his eyes filled with quiet resolve. There was no demon giant. There were no villagers to save. There were only misty memories from bygone days.

At the same time, he was jostled awake from his impromptu slumber by a messenger who was to deliver him to the council of The Destiny of Tyr.

———◆———

The Defiler was still hiding, buried in the heart of the celestial realms. He was a renegade god who had broken free from the realms of glory and had a burning in his heart that he and he alone would rule the realms of men. When the great council rebuked him, the Defiler went mad. He journeyed from world to world, tortured and forced to worship and praise by all children of men.

"They will love me as a god, or I will kill them. None will escape my destiny! We will see who is the greatest of all gods!" screamed the defiant deity.

"I will bring chaos and ruin to all who dare stand in my way," he declared, his voice now a thunderous roar that seemed to shake the foundations of the earth. "I will not rest until every kingdom falls, every city crumbles, and every soul cowers in fear before me!"

This disgraced deity, consumed by madness and bitterness, had set his sights on wreaking havoc upon humanity, throwing the universe into a chaotic imbalance.

As news of the Defiler's escape spread throughout the heavens, the other gods convened to discuss a plan to stop him before he could unleash his wrath upon the mortal realm. Among them was the wise and powerful deity known as Thor, who had long served as the protector of humanity.

"We cannot allow the Defiler to continue unchecked," Thor declared, his voice echoing through the halls of the divine palace. "If we do not stop him, the consequences will be catastrophic."

The other gods murmured in agreement, their faces grim with worry. It was clear that they needed a champion to face the Defiler, someone brave and strong enough to stand against a rogue god.

Thor had heard tales of a fearless warrior named Dragonwülf. Known for his bravery and strength, he was chosen by The Destiny of Tyr to be resurrected from the land of the dead after being killed by an assassin's cross bolt. In exchange for a new life, Dragonwülf agreed to serve the Destiny. The fate of the universe was uncertain, as a renegade God, the Defiler, had disrupted the harmony of existence.

Dragonwülf stood before the panel of beings, his sword gleaming in the dim light of the Great Hall. The leader of The Destiny, the wise Thor with eyes that held the secrets of the cosmos, spoke in a voice that echoed with power.

"Warrior of Arom, you have been chosen for a task of great importance. The renegade god must be stopped before all is lost. Travel back and forward in time, to histories of chaos and despair, and right the wrongs that have been done."

"Is that all? I thought for a moment that the mighty Thor would choose some more difficult task," replied Dragonwülf in a challenging tone." The Destiny of Tyr resurrected an old, dead man. What advantage could you expect to gain? My exploits of bravery in battle are in my past, long since buried with the bones of my vanquished foes."

"We will show you in a dream," said Thor as he placed his gloved hand over the face of the warrior. *"Sleep, old one, and see what you must do."* Dragonwülf's heart pounded with a mix of excitement and trepidation as all around him became dark. He knew the dangers that awaited him, but his honor and duty and his heart compelled him to accept the quest. He fell back into a snowbank and descended into a deep slumber.

The old warrior dreamed a deep dream that he journeyed through the mists of time, and he found himself in a land torn asunder by the wrath of the renegade God. The sky was ashen, the ground barren, and the once proud cities lay in ruins. The air echoed with the cries of the oppressed and the wails of the damned.

Gathering his courage, Dragonwülf set out to track down The Defiler through his murky slumber. In his dream vision, his path was fraught with peril, as servants of the renegade God sought to thwart his progress at every turn. Dragonwülf pressed on, his determination unwavering.

Finally, after many trials and battles, Dragonwülf stood face-to-face with the renegade God. The being towered over him, twisted and malevolent.

"So, the mighty Thor and Destiny of Tyr sends a mere mortal, an old man, a broken-down old fool to challenge me?" the renegade God sneered. "You are but a pawn in their game, Dragonwülf. You cannot hope to defeat me."

Dragonwülf raised his sword, the blade humming with power. "I may be a mortal, but I fight with the strength of my fallen brethren and the courage of the just. I will not falter in my duty, no matter the odds. Bring forth your pain and let me feed upon it!" ordered Dragonwülf.

The battle that followed was a clash of steel and magic echoing across the ravaged landscape. Dragonwülf fought with all his might, his heart filled with the hope of his ancestors.

 As the renegade God lay defeated at his feet, Dragonwülf raised the broad sword over his head, and with all his might, he removed the head of The Defiler. The balance of the universe had been restored, thanks to his bravery and sacrifice.

 The leader of The Destiny of Tyr appeared before Dragonwülf. "Awaken, great warrior," ordered Avat'or. The warrior's eyes opened with pride. "How long have I been in slumber? Did I accomplish my task as I had seen in the vision? Did I vanquish the Defiler and take his head?"

 "No brave warrior, these visions were only planted within you by Thor to show you what may be done in time," explained Avat'or. "He has returned to the heavenly realms. These are only glimpses of the future that you and your crew of resurrected beings must bring to fruition. You can do what few ever will be able to, Dragonwülf. The universe will owe you a debt of gratitude. Your name will be remembered for all time as a hero of the ages.

 We will send you back to your crew aboard your new ship, *Deepwater Watchman*. You will await further instructions from us."

Artifact Six

Salr þjófa
A Gallery Of Rogues

Date: Futuristic Dimension of Höðr (2296)
Unknown kilometers above the Earth and the Under-Forest aboard
The Deepwater Watchman

"Time runs out in the realm. The sinner has run out of time to do wrong. The saint has run out of time to do good deeds. The sinner's closet is full of bleached, dead men's bones mixed with the bones of the saints."
-Dr. Albert Moreau

Each member of the crew of the Deepwater was chosen for a specific purpose, their unique abilities to shape the fate of worlds. Each member had agreed to a resurrection from death in return for serving at the orders of the leaders of the Destiny of Tyr. On this day, they would all tell their tales.

The new leader was Dragonwülf, a fierce warrior unmatched on the field of battle. His strength and courage made him a formidable force, feared by enemies and revered by allies.

"I am Dragonwülf, a mere mortal blessed by the gods with strength and courage," he began, his words carrying a humble air that belied his towering stature and fearsome reputation. "I have faced countless foes on the battlefield, from frost giants in the north to mighty dragons in the west. Yet I do not boast of my victories, for I know that they were won with the aid of Óðinn, Thor, Róthul-Orkr, and my fellow members of the Destiny of Tyr. I have faced the fury of my enemies and emerged victorious, not through my own strength alone, but through the bonds of brotherhood that unite us all," Dragonwülf declared, his eyes beaming with a fierce light.

"I can tell you that this man has not always been so humble," said Captain Old-Turas, who was at the wheel of the great ship. "It took him getting a cross-bolt in the neck to humble him."

"That may be a true old one, but I am still a humble servant of the gods, a warrior who walks the path of duty and honor," he said, his voice soft yet filled with an undeniable strength.

Jarvis Nightwish from Saturn Moon Enceladus Colony was one chosen by the Destiny of Tyr, selected for his ruthless efficiency as an executioner. His cold demeanor and unwavering dedication to his duty made him a force to be reckoned with. Jarvis carried out his tasks with precision and without hesitation *until* he developed a conscience.

"My fellow travelers, my name is Jarvis Nightwish, and I am the hand of justice in a forsaken place," he spoke, his voice low and gravelly. "I did what had to be done, without hesitation or remorse."

His eyes, sharp and cold like shards of ice, held a flash of something darker, something primal. Jarvis was a man who felt peace in his role, finding solace in the act of delivering justice to those who dared to defy the laws of the Holy Temple of the Saturn Moon Enceladus Colony.

"I have watched as the guilty tremble before me, begging for mercy they do not deserve," Jarvis continued, his words dripping with disdain. "But mercy is a luxury I cannot afford. I am the instrument of the temple's will, and I am unyielding in my resolve. I am no hero, no savior," Jarvis declared, his tone unapologetic. "I am the Enceladus temple executioner, and I do what must be done to maintain order and balance in this sacred place."

"How can you justify death in the name of a strange and fictitious religion?" asked a confused Sir Robert Winterfall, the 19th-century archeologist. "What could these poor people have done to deserve such a ghastly fate?"

"I have faced Kings and paupers alike, their cries for mercy falling on deaf ears," Jarvis declared, his icy blue eyes glinting with a steely resolve. "None can escape the swift justice of the Temple of Enceladus, for in the end, all must answer for their sins. I must admit their screams have cut through me like a knife, and I decided to only kill those who have richly earned such a fate."

"A repentant killer?

"Call me what you will, but I will redeem myself," said Nightwish. "I discovered only much too late that the so-called High Priest Xemias, who demanded death as repentance. He was nothing more than a masquerade of the high priest. I hope he rots in Hades."

Another assassin, Viktor Vorobyev, was chosen for his cunning and ruthless nature, his skills as a killer honed through years of murder and crime. He moved through the shadows like a wraith, striking fear into the hearts of those who dared to cross his path.

Viktor chuckled, a sound that sent shivers down the spine of those around him. "I will tell you a story," he said, his tone low and menacing. "Once, I was riding through the desert on my trusty steed, my Harley-Davidson as it roared beneath me. I came across a gang of bandits terrorizing a small town, and I knew I had to take action. I just hate bullies."

As Viktor spoke, his hands moved animatedly, his eyes glinting with a fierce light. The group hung on his every word, unable to tear their eyes away from the imposing figure before them. "I stood up those dirt bags and let me tell you, they never knew what hit 'em," Viktor continued, a wicked grin spreading across his face. "I took them down one by one with some badass shotgun blasts. Don't judge me, they had it comin'."

Viktor then settled back in his chair, the air around him charged with a potent mix of reverence and fear." I will kill the first one of you that crosses me, I promise that… so keep your distance."

The crew was introduced to Luciano Cantore, a master of deception and manipulation. He was chosen for his connections to organized crime. As a skilled hitman, he carried out his murders with precision. Luciano's ability to navigate the criminal underworld made him a valuable asset until he was murdered in a gangland hit by his brother.

"You act like you're the only guy who could ever kill anybody, dude," Luciano said to Viktor, the biker. "I am not impressed. Let me tell you one of my best hits," Luciano began his voice low and gravelly. "It was the time I was hired to take out Don Salvatore's right-hand man, Tony 'The Blade' Moretti. The guy was known for his quick reflexes and skilled knife work, but I managed to get the drop on him. Never bring a knife to a gun fight," he laughed, a chilling laugh.

As Luciano spoke, his face looked like a dangerous light, reliving the adrenaline of the moment. The other passengers of the ship leaned in, hanging on his every word.

"I followed Tony for days, studying his movements and habits," Luciano continued. "One night, as he was leaving a high-end restaurant, I made my move. I stepped out of the shadows, gun in hand, and before he even knew what hit him, Tony was lying on the ground, bleeding out. No more Tony. I also hit the mayor of Sicily himself," Luciano said, his voice filled with pride. "The man had surrounded himself with layers of security, making it nearly impossible to get close to him. I am not called 'The Ghost' for nothing. I disguised myself as a janitor, slipping past the guards unnoticed. When the mayor least expected it, I struck. A single bullet to the head, right between his freakin' eyes, and the most powerful man in Sicily was just a bag of guts. Just in case you think I got away with something, a few years later, my own brother set me up, and those traitors in Chicago whacked me. I guess that's how I ended up here," said Luciano. "Nobody ever gets away with nothin',"

Captain Santiago Old-Turas, a vengeful spirit with unparalleled ship piloting skills, was chosen by the Destiny of Tyr for his thirst for revenge and unwavering loyalty. His cunning tactics and strategic mind made him a formidable leader, and his crew followed him into battle without question. Old-Turas' skill in piloting ships through treacherous space made him a force to be reckoned with, his determination driving him forward against all odds. He met his match when Ingegärd the Witch Queen created a mammoth dragon named Ghidorwrath. Captain Old-Turas stood at the helm of his new ship, the Deepwater Watchman, his weathered face solemn as the memories of his past haunted him. "I'll never forget that fateful day," he began, his voice filled with emotion. "The day the North Hundren and its brave crew were taken from me by Ghidorwrath, the serpent.

His crew listened intently, their eyes wide with curiosity as Captain Old-Turas recounted the events that had led to his thirst for revenge. "We were sailing through a treacherous sky, the wind howling and crashing against our hull," he continued, his voice growing stronger with each word. "That's when Ghidorwrath emerged from Hades, its eyes filled with malice and its scales gleaming in the moonlight."

The North Hundren fought bravely against the monstrous serpent. "We fought with all our might, but Ghidorwrath was too powerful," he said, his eyes burning with determination. "In the end, my beloved ship was torn asunder, and my crew... my friends... they were lost to death. Later, Dragonwülf and his army destroyed Ghidorwrath. The Witch Queen lives on and must be found!"

Tears welled up in the Captain's eyes as he vowed to seek vengeance upon the creator of the giant serpent that had brought him such sorrow. "I have spent years searching for the Witch Queen, tracking her movements and honing my skills as a sailor and a warrior," he declared, his voice echoing with resolve. "Now, with the Deepwater Watchman at my command, I will have my revenge."

As the Deepwater Watchman sailed away from the safety of the harbor, Captain Old-Turas stood tall at the helm, his eyes fixed on the horizon. The wind whispered through the sails, carrying with it a sense of anticipation and excitement. The crew knew that they were embarking on a dangerous adventure, but they also knew that they were united in their quest for justice. With Captain Old-Turas leading the way, they were prepared to face whatever trials awaited them on the open sea. Sir Robert Winterfall, a scholar of time travel and archeology, was chosen for the crew for his knowledge and expertise in uncovering ancient secrets. His studies and discoveries shaped the Destiny of Tyr's understanding of the galaxy and its history, his insights guiding them toward their ultimate goals. Winterfall's thirst for knowledge and unyielding curiosity made him a vital member of this ancient race, his discoveries unlocking mysteries long forgotten.

"I have seen wonders beyond imagination," Sir Winterfall began, his voice filled with passion. "Beneath the very floor of Norway lies the remnants of an ancient civilization—one that predates even the Vikings themselves."

The room fell silent as the group leaned in, captivated by Sir Winterfall's words. He described the intricate carvings and towering structures he had uncovered, the artifacts that spoke of a culture long forgotten. As he spoke, a shadow of sadness crossed his face.

"No one believes me," he lamented. "They say I have gone mad, that I have fabricated these tales for fame and glory. Now, everyone aboard the ship can see for themselves what I say is true. Our leader Dragonwülf comes from this land!"

In the dark corner of the ship, there lurked a figure so gruesome and terrifying that his very name sent shivers down the spine of anyone who dared to speak of him. Hansel Gru'el, or as he was known, The Harvester of Eyes, was a being with a sinister purpose that struck fear into the hearts of all who crossed his path.

Terrified, they turned to see a tall figure standing before them, cloaked in shadows and emanating a blinding ray of evil. His eyes, or what appeared to be eyes, glowed with an otherworldly light that pierced through the darkness.

"I am cursed to see the darkest depths of the human heart, to bear the burden of every soul's pain and suffering. But with your eyes, I can see into your mind and understand the true nature of your humanity... or your inhumanity."

Leaning on a yardarm in the aft of the ship, just barely visible from the others, was Zachariah Boyd, a nineteenth-century cowboy and gunslinger. "I got brought here by the Destiny after I got hung for killin' a cheatin' drover during a card game. I am good with my pistols, and I am a good poker player. I don't know why else the fancy destiny dudes would want me."

Together, these chosen members of Destiny shaped the fate of the galaxy, their actions reverberating through the stars and influencing the course of history.

The gallery of rogues of the Destiny of Tyr was assembled on the deck of their ship, and the icy wind sliced through them like an assassin's blade as they gathered to recount their heroic episodes. Captain Old-Turas, the fearless ship captain with a glint of adventure in his eyes, called a meeting to order.

"Friends," Old-Turas began, "we have faced many challenges on our journey. It is in these moments of trial that our true heroism shines. Let us each share a tale of our bravery and valor."

"And what about you, Captain? Dragonwülf asked, turning to the old sea dog. "Surely you have a tale of heroism to share with us?"

Amid a meager crew and the Destiny of Tyr, Captain Old-Turas sat by the ship's wheel with a tankard of ale in hand. His weathered face told tales of voyages across the tumultuous seas, and his eyes twinkled with the fire of a thousand sunsets.

"Ah, ye want to hear a tale of heroism on the high seas, do ye?" Captain Old-Turas boomed in his gravelly voice, capturing the attention of everyone on the ship. The patrons nodded enthusiastically, eager to listen to the legendary captain's story.

"Many years ago, my brave crew and I set sail on the *North Hundren* in search of the fabled Isle of Whispers," Old-Turas began, his words weaving a vivid tapestry of the unknown waters in which they ventured. "We faced storms that could swallow ships whole, and monsters that lurked beneath the waves, but we never wavered in our quest. And then, on the darkest night of our journey, a night much like this one," he began, his voice carrying the weight of years of experience. "The wind was fierce, and the waves rose and fell like the chests of sleeping giants. We were sailing through the treacherous waters of the Dragon's Maw, our ship cutting through the darkness like a knife through butter. We encountered the dreaded Jörmungandr," Captain Old-Turas exclaimed, his eyes glinting with a mixture of fear and determination. "Its tentacles rose from the depths, threatening to drag us down into the abyss. Then it happened!" His audience leaned in, captivated by the promise of an epic tale. Captain Old-Turas took a sip of rum before continuing, his eyes wandering into the distant past.

"As we battled against the raging tempest, a man's scream tore through me like a dagger had been pierced through the howling winds." Man overboard!" rang out across the deck, sending shivers down my old spine."

A hush fell over the deck as the captain paused for dramatic effect, his gaze sweeping over his spellbound audience.

"I braved the crashing waves and thundering skies, determined to rescue my fallen crewman. With a roar that could rival the storm itself, I plunged into the icy waters, the salt spray stinging my skin. The crew watched in awe as I fought against the powerful currents, my muscles straining with every stroke."

"You're one brave soul, old chap!" exclaimed Dr. Winterfall, his eyes wide with admiration.

"Bravery comes from within," replied Captain Old-Turas with a not-so-humble nod. "But it was not just courage that saved the day. After what seemed like an eternity, I finally reached our fallen comrade and pulled him to safety with my one good arm, swimming as fast as I could. With my other arm, I jabbed two fingers into the eye of the bloody Jörmungandr. He screamed like the beastie coward he was and then slunk back into the deep. I yelled, if you want more of that, I have plenty for ya!

The crew cheered as I made my way back to the safety of the ship."

As the last echoes of his tale faded away, Captain Old-Turas raised his tankard in a silent toast to the heroes of the high seas, his eyes sparkling with pride and nostalgia.

Dragonwülf chuckled within himself, knowing the actual story of the rescued crewmember. He would never tell. As the last echoes of the tale faded into the night, Captain Old-Turas leaned back in his chair with a satisfied smile; his eyes twinkling with the memories of a life well lived on the high seas.

As the sun began to set on the horizon, casting a golden glow over the gathering of heroes, they raised their voices in a toast to the destiny that brought them together.

Dragonwülf cleared his throat, the sound echoing through the chamber. "Welcome, aboard, you band of salty rogues," he began, his voice like thunder. "We are gathered here today to unravel the mysteries of our origins and the purpose bestowed upon us by the ancient alien race, Destiny of Tyr."

Jarvis Nightwish stepped forward, his metallic weapon, the disruptor, clinking softly. "I have long sought answers to the questions that plague my mind," he said, his voice low and steady. "Tell us, Dragonwülf, what is it that Destiny of Tyr requires of us?"

Dragonwülf's eyes glittered with ancient wisdom as he spoke. "I know that all of us have been given the task of reconciling our own history. *They wish us to correct our wrongs. A second chance has been given to us after our deaths.* The Destiny of Tyr has foreseen a Great War looming on the horizon, a battle that will shake the very foundations of the cosmos. We are chosen to stand together, to unite our strengths and abilities, to protect the realms from the encroaching darkness. We can only balance the universe by reconciling ours."

"You mean righting *our* wrongs, not just the world's wrongs? I guess I had this figured all wrong?" asked Luciano.

"I never saw any need for any kind of repentance. It just ain't my style," said Viktor through a sneer.

"I'm with him on that. No absolution from a priest is gonna wipe clean the stuff I did," said Luciano in a rough Chicago Italian Accent.

Viktor snorted derisively. "I am no saint, and I certainly ain't sorry for what I did," he sneered, his hand resting casually on the hilt of his blade. "I kill for *my* reasons, not for anybody else."

"Destiny does not require absolution! They only *require* balance. You must balance good with evil. It is required of your resurrection. To do that, we may have to have the blood of evil ones on our hands, but we will never cause the innocent to suffer," said Dragonwülf.

"Innocent people die in war; it is just an eternal truth," said the Captain.

"By the name of all of our gods, they will not die at our hands, so help me," said Dragonwülf.

Luciano chuckled darkly, tipping his fedora. "We *all* got lots of blood on our hands, Viktor. But maybe this thing might be bigger than any one of us."

Captain Old-Turas nodded solemnly. "Aye, we may be a rough-looking crew, but together I think we can make any enemy run and hide."

Zachariah Boyd spoke up, his voice gruff. "I've faced my fair share of fights, but this... this feels different. Like we're fightin' somethin' we can't see."

Ser Robert Winterfall scribbled furiously in his notes, capturing the essence of their conversation for posterity.

Viktor snorted his cynical smirk, cutting through the gravity of the moment. "I ain't anybody's puppet," he sneered, crossing his arms defiantly. "I make my own fate, no alien overlords gonna tell me otherwise."

"You do not understand, you simple-minded horse's ass! You have no choice! Destiny will return you to the dark hole from which you came. Your headless corpse will be a testament to your stubbornness," said Dragonwülf as a stern warning.

Viktor stared intently with his hand on his switchblade within an icy glare of death.

"I would not do that if I were you. Your blade will not reach me before you are struck dead and returned to your tomb," warned Dragonwülf.

Viktor thought better of his plan and removed his hand from his blade.

Luciano raised an eyebrow, his gaze cold and calculating. "Perhaps, my friend, but even the most ruthless among us cannot deny the pull of destiny."

Captain Old-Turas slammed his tankard on the table, his eyes shining with a fierce resolve. "Well, whether we're pawns or kings in this game, I say we all play our parts well! You never know, this might be more fun than we figured!"

"Very well said, Captain!" said Dragonwülf.

Zachariah Boyd tipped his hat, excitement in his eyes. "I reckon it is gonna be one hell of a ride, but by the grace of the Almighty, we'll face whatever comes our way."

Sir Robert Winterfall raised his quill, a glimmer of scholarly curiosity in his eyes. "Let the chronicles of Dragonwülf and the Destiny of Tyr be written for all time.

Artifact Seven

Dreki skugglands

ᛞᚱᛖᚲᛁ ᛊᚲᚢᚷᚷᛚᚨᚾᛞᛊ

(Dragnon Shadowland)

Date: Dimension of Höðr (2296) BCE

"Augun hans brunnu með óhelgum eldi, hinn áður blíði rómr hans var nú hvísl ógnar sem ómaði um tómið."

FUGUT HFTE BRUTTU

MMB UHMFXUM MFWI

HIT FUMUR BFIWI RQMR HFTE

PFR TU PPIET QXTFR

EMM QHFWI UM TQMIM

"His eyes burned with an unholy fire, his once gentle voice now a menacing whisper that echoed through the void."

In the cosmic realm of gods and celestial beings, there existed a benevolent deity known as Dragnon Shadowland. He was revered for his compassion, his wisdom, and his unwavering commitment to justice. Dragnon was beloved by all who dwelled in the vast expanse of the universe. His presence brought peace and harmony wherever he went.

Dragnon's benevolence was not without its consequences. The council of gods realized his power and influence and grew concerned. They feared that worship of this being would corrupt him by overshadowing the mission of the gods. Soon, his adoration did encompass him with pride and caused him to demand all the worship for himself alone. The council of gods decided to cast him out, to strip him of his divinity and leave him to roam the galaxy alone for eternity. The council of the Old Gods sent for Shadowland to appear before them.

He stood imposing in the center of the grand hall, his dark cloak billowing around him like a stormy cloud. His piercing gaze fixed on the council of gods before him, their faces mired in anger. The air was filled with tension as they faced off in a battle of wills that would shape the fate of the cosmos.

Höðr, the leader of the tribunal, a wise and ancient deity, stepped forward, his voice like the whisper of the wind through the leaves. "Shadowland, your power has grown beyond measure, and we can no longer ignore the threat you pose to the balance of the universe. It is because of this that we are assigning you to the realms of the lands of death, the region of Hel."

He scoffed, "Jealousy does not become you, old man. Perhaps if you spent less time squabbling amongst yourselves and more time attending to your duties, you would not fear my influence."

A murmur rippled through the assembled gods, their eyes flashing with anger at this god's insolence. Höðr raised a hand, urging them to remain calm.

"We are not here to quarrel, but to find a resolution to this growing conflict. Your actions have consequences, and we cannot allow you to jeopardize the fragile peace we have fought so hard to maintain."

Shadowland's lips curled into a cruel smile, his eyes squinting with anger. "Peace is an illusion, *fool*. The universe is *my* canvas waiting to be painted with chaos and destruction. I am the eternal artist who will draw you unto your doom. My power is beyond your comprehension, and you would do well to remember that."

Höðr's expression hardened, his blind eyes trying to understand the inconceivable. "We may not have your raw power, but we have something far more potent. We stand together as one, bound by duty and honor, while you stand alone in your quest for dominion. It is time to choose your path. Do you wish to continue down this terrible path, or will you turn back?"

"You do not understand the genius of my master plan. Our subjects excuse me …my subjects love and adore me. I would never do anything to hurt them. As soon as their weak, foolish adoration is at its peak, that is when I strike. I will hit them with all of their lies, hypocrisy, and even their own violence and bring them to their knees. You can share in this with me as my fellows, or you will serve me."

Höðr slammed his heavy gavel on the table. "Seize him and cast him down! We must be free of this terrible influence on our people."

The renegade god let out a low, menacing laugh that sent shivers down the spines of the council members. "I have made my choice. I will not be swayed by weak-willed fools such as you. Prepare yourselves for the storm that is to come! I will not rest until I have conquered all that lies before me! See me in your fearful nightmares and know me from this day forward as "The Defiler of Souls!"

What he saw as the council's betrayal cut deep into his heart, turning his once kind soul into one filled with darkness and rage. As he was cast into the outer darkness, he felt the weight of his newfound exile bearing down on him. The once benevolent god now called himself death and revenge incarnate, vowed vengeance on the universe that had rejected him.

Alone in the cold emptiness of space, Defiler's mind was twisted and warped, consumed by thoughts of revenge. He wandered the galaxy, his once majestic form now twisted and distorted by the darkness that had engulfed him. His eyes burned with an unholy fire, his once gentle voice now a menacing whisper that echoed through the void.

"I am The Defiler of Souls," he cried out into the abyss. "I will have my revenge on those who have wronged me. The council of gods will pay for their treachery, and the universe will know the wrath of one cast out from its divine embrace."

His words reverberated through the cosmos, a dark omen of the chaos to come. His rage fueled him, driving him to seek out those who had betrayed him and bring upon them a reckoning like no other. His once noble purpose twisted into a desire for destruction, a thirst for vengeance that could never be quenched.

In the fiery depths of Hel, the Defiler ventured forth with a sinister purpose in mind. His malevolent gaze swept across the tortured souls that writhed and screamed in agony as he searched for those who would serve him in his vessel to carry his evil purpose to the galaxies. His dark armor glinted menacingly in the flickering light of the eternal flames that surrounded him, a testament to the power and cruelty he possessed.

Approaching a group of demons who cowered before him, the Defiler spoke, and his mouth drooled with the blood of lost souls.

"I seek servants who will aid me in my quest to build a ship that will traverse the universe to serve as a planet destroyer. Who among you is willing to join me in this endeavor?"

The demons quivered in fear, but one, a towering figure with horns that curled menacingly, stepped forward. "I will serve you, my lord," he growled, his eyes glowing with a malevolent light. "What must I do?"

The Defiler smirked, his twisted lips curling into a cruel smile. "Gather the finest minds and the most skilled artisans of Hell," he commanded. "We will build a ship unlike any that has ever existed, equipped with modern weapons systems that will strike fear into the hearts of all who oppose us. We will show the gods what minds they have locked in Hell for all eternity. Only then will it be too late for them to be sorry for what they have done."

The demons set to work, their dark energies fueling the construction of the ship that would bring devastation to worlds beyond imagination. The Defiler oversaw every detail, his mind teeming with dark visions of destruction and chaos.

As the ship neared completion, the Defiler stood before his assembled servants, his gaze filled with triumph. "At last, our weapon is ready," he declared. "Now, we shall unleash it upon the unsuspecting creatures of the universe and watch as they fall before us."

The demons cheered, their cries echoing through the fiery caverns of Hell. With a triumphant laugh, He boarded the spaceship, his servants at his side, and set a course for the first world on their path of destruction.

The planet destroyer sailed out into the void, a harbinger of doom and despair, and its weapons primed and ready to unleash devastation upon all who dared to defy the will of The Defiler.

"Well done, my servants! Once we launch, we will be invincible! *I will* be unstoppable in my power!" the Defiler gloated. All will know the name of the planet destroyer, *The Götterdämmerung*, The Twilight of the Gods! Their time has come!"

Dragnon Shadowland's path of destruction left planets in ruins, civilizations in despair, and the council of gods trembling in fear. The universe had rejected him. The Defiler would make sure that it remembered his name for eternity.

The Destiny of Tyr

The God Tyr, the god of weapons and war, sought to put together a council of beings to pursue balance in the universe. He called them The Destiny of Tyr.

The Destiny of Tyr, tasked with upholding justice across the cosmos, had made it their solemn mission to put an end to the Defiler's reign of terror as it began. With hearts pure and spirits strong, they pursued the malevolent god relentlessly, their determination unwavering despite the countless obstacles in their path until they were able to follow him to Morak the Under-Sea in the Kingdom of Arom. The Defiler had sought an audience with the then King Draknorr of the Hrothgorn Kingdom.

"You cannot stop me, fools," the Defiler sneered, his voice a chilling whisper that sent shivers down the spines of the brave beings before him. "I am beyond your reach, beyond your comprehension. I am the darkness that lurks in the hearts of all beings, the shadow that blots out the light of hope. Look into your hearts. I am there. I am the evil you wish to hide from the world. I am that private spot in your twisted, lustful, arrogant, and greedy minds that you say does not exist. It does, and you revel in it when no one is watching you."

The Destiny of Tyr would not be swayed by his words of deceit and manipulation. With a strength born of righteousness and courage forged in the fires of adversity, they advanced upon the Defiler, their weapons drawn and their hearts filled with determination.

"You may be a god of darkness and despair," spoke Avat'or the, his voice steady and unwavering. "But we are beings of light and justice, sworn to protect the innocent and uphold the balance of the universe. You will not escape us this time, Defiler. Your reign of terror ends here."

The Defiler laughed a sound that echoed through the barren wasteland like the howl of a dying beast. "You may have courage, but I am eternal, unstoppable. I am the end of all things."

With a flash of blinding light and a clash of thunderous power, The Defiler unleashed his dark magic upon the valiant beings that stood against him, his spells twisting the very fabric of reality and unleashing chaos upon them. With a wave of powerful energy and one wave of his gnarled hand, he sent the Destiny of Tyr crashing to the valley floor below. He laughed with a disturbing cadence as he watched them fall to their doom.

The skies turned black with storm clouds, and the ground shook as the Defiler was able to escape into a dimension unknown and faded from view.

Tyr appeared to the shattered corpses of the Destiny of Tyr on the sea bottom. "Arise! Your work is not done. I will return you to your former state. You will not taste of death until you have earned it."

The brave souls of the Destiny arose from the muck of the deep and rose to the surface. Avat'or shook the mud from his robes and surveyed all around him, realizing he was not allowed to die, and released an epithet from his soul.

"Blorthe!" This essentially means in English, 'Dammit, not this again.'

Artifact Eight

Rökr goðanna

The Twilight of the Gods

Date: Dimension of Höðr (2296) CE

"Vér stöndum á brún opinberunar er mun endurmynda skilning vár á sögu ok staðr vár í vef heimsins."

ᚹᛖᚱ ᛊᛏᚢᛗᚢᛗᛖ ᚠ ᛒᚱᚢᛏ ᛦᚲᛁᛏᛒᛖᚱᚢᛏᚠᚱ

ᛗᚱ ᛗᚢᛏ ᛖᛏᛗᚢᚱᛗᛁᛏᛗᚠ ᛊᚲᛁᚱᛏᛁᛏᚷ ᚹᚠᚱ

ᚠ ᛊᛟᚷᚢ ᛟᚲ ᛊᛏᚠᚹᚱ ᚹᚠᚱ ᛁ ᚹᛖᚹ ᚺᛖᛁᛗᛊᛁᛏᛊ

"*We stand on the brink of a revelation that will reshape our understanding of history and our place in the tapestry of the world.*"

In the dimension of Höðr, home to gods and warriors alike, Dragonwülf was summoned to the celestial realm directly from the deck of the Deepwater Watchman.

"Come forth, Dragonwülf, you who has the blood of dragons, the son of all who reside with him, arise!"

"How in the name of Hades do you get me here? I have never been to the Celestial realm," said a slightly agitated Dragonwülf. "You could have just called me without all of the flowery, unnecessary words. I am not special."

Tyr, the god of war, stood before Dragonwülf with a grave expression on his face.

"The time has come, Dragonwülf," Tyr spoke with urgency in his voice. "The Defiler has risen, and his killer planet, The Götterdämmerung, looms on the horizon. The fate of all realms hangs in the balance."

Dragonwülf's eyes blazed with determination.

"One day, I wandered into the Hall of the Ancients, a broken old man, and now I hold the fate of the universe. It rests in my hands as a member of The Destiny of Tyr. I pray to Róthul-Orkr that I can be worthy of what I have been entrusted with. I pray that I might continue my journey to Valhalla some bright day. My journey for Tyr seems to have no beginning or end. Tell me what I must do. I have agreed to interrupt my death and my journey to Valhalla."

"Dragonwülf, you are our last hope against The Defiler. But be warned, he is a foe unlike any other, born from the darkest depths of the universe."

"I feel as though I have been misled! Why in the name of Róthul-Orkr am I your Last hope?" argued Dragonwülf now in the presence of The Destiny of Tyr. The assortment of ancient beings stood before him on the deck of the ship. Dragonwulf had agreed to be resurrected in exchange for undying Service to the Destiny.

"I would never have agreed to do battle with an unbeatable foe such as that… *gutter-rung* behemoth thing! I cannot say the thing because my tongue cannot surround the word. I told Tyr I was not special."

The leader of the Destiny interrupted, "That is the *Götterdämmerung*, the killer of planets. The threat of Hrothgorn, the Witch Queen, or any earthly calamity must bow down to the threat from The Defiler and his creation. We must all face this titan and send it to the pits of Hel from whence it came. This is why we seek your wisdom. There is no bigger threat to the Defiler than you. The most brilliant minds and powerful sorcerers came together to devise a plan, but there is no replacement for your skills in defeating the renegade deity."

"I am your faithful servant and always at your command, mighty Tyr," promised Dragonwülf

Die Götterdämmerung

The Defiler chose this name, meaning The Twilight of the Gods, to label a horrible means of destruction with an elegant misnomer. It was the size of most planets and was on a collision course with our galaxy, set in motion by the renegade Defiler. He was able to move from dimension to dimension by throwing himself into the Panorama of time as it passed in review like soldiers marching past the Götterdämmerung.

The Defiler sought to conquer and destroy, using his unparalleled knowledge of cosmic forces to lay waste to civilizations across the universe.

It was not enough for him to annihilate his enemies. He craved an event of cataclysmic proportions, one that would etch his name into the history of the cosmos forever. He conjured a weapon unlike anything ever before seen - The Götterdämmerung. In the vast expanse of the universe, where stars were born and galaxies flourished, there existed a formidable entity known as The Götterdämmerung. This colossal planet-sized entity was not merely a destroyer of galaxies, but a bringer of chaos and terror across the cosmos. It was inhabited by The Defiler, a being of immense power and darkness, along with his legion of malevolent demons.

The Götterdämmerung was unlike anything ever witnessed before. Its surface was a swirling maelstrom of shadows and crimson hues as if the very essence of evil itself had taken form. Lightning crackled across its surface, illuminating the grotesque features of twisted spires and jagged cliffs that dotted its landscape. Rivers of molten lava snaked their way through the desolate terrain, casting an eerie glow upon the infernal landscape.

In the center of the Götterdämmerung, the Defiler sat perched upon his self-built molten throne, his eyes burning with a fire that struck fear into the hearts of all who beheld him. His twisted form was shrouded in darkness, his skin a sickly hue that seemed to absorb the very light around him. His claws were as sharp as daggers, and his fangs gleamed with a seething hunger that terrified all present.

The Defiler's army of grotesque creatures with twisted faces roamed the surface of The Götterdämmerung like a plague. Their howls echoed through the darkened skies, sending shivers down the spines of those who dared to approach. They were relentless in their pursuit of chaos and destruction, carrying out the Defiler's bidding with a fervor that knew no bounds.

People throughout the universe whispered of The Götterdämmerung's insatiable thirst for annihilation, its hunger for the destruction of entire galaxies. It was said that when The Defiler unleashed the full power of his hate, worlds trembled and stars fell from the heavens. None who had dared to challenge its might had lived to tell the tale, for The Götterdämmerung was a force of nature beyond comprehension.

The Götterdämmerung lingered in the darkest corners of the universe, a forerunner of doom and despair, a colossal entity of destruction and chaos that cast a shadow over all who beheld it. Its very presence was a testament to the eternal evil within.

The monstrosity cast a haunting, ghostly shadow over the galaxies it passed. It was a sinister blend of violet, crimson, and emerald, sent shivers down the spines of all who witnessed it. It was as though the very fabric of reality was being torn in two.

The Destiny embarked on a perilous mission to confront the dark forces threatening to plunge the universe into eternal darkness.

Dragonwulf's band of misfits made their way to the heart of the chaos, where The Defiler awaited them. He sought to shroud the universe in eternal darkness, feeding on the despair and fear of all living beings. The search for the Götterdämmerung had begun.

In the heart of his sinister fortress, the Defiler had long awaited news of Avat'or of the Destiny's capture. Swiftly, his creatures ambushed the unsuspecting leader and brought him before their wicked master. His eyes, red with rage, gleamed through a narrow slit in a helmet forged of iron. Spines protruded from the helmet much like antlers. His face was covered by a mask that left his jaw uncovered. Flames flickered from underneath his chest plate and shimmered from his forearms. The Defiler was regaled with a giant iron wingspan that smoked as if it had been recently forged.

The Defiler's demons had captured Avat'or, the Grand leader of the Destiny of Tyr.

"You *know* where the scum known as The Destiny of Tyr is hidden! Reveal them to me. Your answer will decide your fate," demanded The Defiler to his helpless prisoner. "When you look into my eyes, what do you see?"

"I see evil, empty eyes full of hate and nothing more."

Flying into a rage, the defiler raked his clawed fingers into the prisoner's eyes.

"What do you see now, you pitiful wretch?" said the Defiler as his victim emitted a painful, tortured scream.

Avat'or, the leader of The Destiny of Tyr, was subjected to the brutality of the bloody torture chamber at the hands of The Defiler. With his sinister powers and endless thirst for dominance, The Defiler unleashed chaos and frantic, unthinkable pain on Avat'or, and his bloody fangs ran red with seething anger and hate.

"Woe unto them who challenge me and the power of my might and strength. Will I show mercy unto those who bend the knee? That makes me tremble with laughter. I intend no mercy for man or beast. I will kill you all!" said The Defiler.

"Your sickening babbling is the worst of your tortures. I can bear it no more. Shut your mouth and stab me with a hot poker or something," said Avat'or, sarcastically trying to see through the blood in his eyes.

"Your jest will stick in your throat like sand!" said The Defiler as he dragged his clawed hand across his prisoner's face. Wounds opened like springs of bloody water.

"The Destiny of Tyr will find you and destroy you. The longer you torment me, the greater the chance they will find you. You cannot hide forever."

"That is exactly what I had hoped. Destiny will come to me and save me some extra toil," said The Defiler. "Your hope that you and Destiny can change history to bring it back into balance is a fool's errand."

"We will see that the wrongs you have done to disturb the balance of the universe are altered and reconciled no matter the cost!' promised Avat'or.

"It is the hypocrisy of the violent world that has set it into imbalance! I have done nothing but witness the ruin of the ages! The people have done this to themselves, and I will see that they pay! What is your plan? Speak to me about your doctrine?" The Defiler asked ironically, taunting his prisoner. "I have had enough of your talk…reveal the Destiny to me!"

"They do not hide. They seek you because you are the prey!" said Avat'or.

"You are a puny, worthless creature! Reveal to me what you keep in your heart," said The Defiler. His voice dripped with bitterness. "If you choose not to surrender your strategies to me, I will snatch the secrets from your heart after I tear it from your chest. How do you intend to bring about my destruction? Your efforts will bring nothing but *pain and blood* to you and the entire Destiny of Tyr. You are indeed a fool."

Avat'or, refusing to succumb to fear, stared defiantly at his captor. "You will never learn of our plans, because we would all gladly suffer death than succumb to you. Rake my flesh, and even then I will never speak what you wish to hear."

"I am so relieved to hear you say that. I have given a painful gift to those in the past, but I will present it to you today. I am so pleased to share it with you. It is one of my beloved creations. It is called *Death by a Thousand Cuts*," hissed the Defiler. Filthy thieves in the Eastern world have taken credit for it, the fools stole it from me, but it belongs to me and no other."

It was then that Avat'or realized the true nature of his adversary's desperation. The Defiler, consumed by fear and paranoia, believed that the Destiny of Tyr possessed the means to defeat him. Avat'or's unwavering resilience was a testament to the strength of his cause. "Do what you will," said Avat'or. "My spirit is ironclad!"

Angered by Avat'or's defiance, the Defiler grinned darkly, revealing his razor-sharp teeth. "You misunderstand. It is not only your flesh that shall suffer the worst of my torments, but your mind and spirit as well."

"Your words fall on deaf ears. You speak rubbish," said Avat'or tauntingly.

"Sometimes I am so clever with my words, I even impress myself," said the Defiler. "Please pardon my rude behavior," he added sarcastically. "Face death now! Let me see the fear smeared on your face along with your blood!"

"I fear death as any man would do, but I do not fear you," said Avat'or, essentially sealing his fate. "You are simply not that terrifying. You have a countenance much like a circus clown, frightening, yes, but still a clown."

The ghoul reacted, screamed in anger, lacerated, and ripped the flesh of the leader, spilling blood over the front of his tunic and onto the floor. Over the shrieks produced from the raw throat of Avat'or, the sounds of maniacal laughter added to the madness of the scene. As the lifeblood of Avat'or dropped from the fanged monster, he spat blood droplets and screeched an evil celebration, reveling in his depravity.

"I will leave this mark on you as a reminder to all," said the Defiler as he raised a glowing, red-hot branding iron. "Do you know what a torture tattoo looks like? It looks painful, but blends in the flesh like an attacker waiting in an ambush. The mark looks like knives and razors. They can even look like other weapons, but they are just ink and nothing more. Do not sleep or even close your eyes in the presence of a torture tattoo. The torture begins when sleep abounds. Rest well, my enemy!"

Avat'or did not yield even as his eyes closed in death as the iron pressed into his flesh, producing the mark of the Defiler, one single lightning bolt.

Later, the Destiny of Tyr rescued Avat'or's corpse from the Saturn Moon Enceladus Colony, where it had been hastily disposed of near the dark forest of Enceladus. He stood up in the pile of refuse and brushed off his robes.

"Dammit, not again," he complained. There was to be no rest at this time for the leader of the Destiny of Tyr. There was much work to be done for this immortal being as Destiny brought him back into their fellowship.

Artifact Nine

Djúpvatsvörðr

ᚺᚨᚠᛗᛊᚾᚳᛖᛈᛟᚱᛗᚱ

The Deepwater Watchman

Date: Future Dimension of Höðr (2296 CE)

"Gold and silver have never done anything useful save to fill my pockets and weigh me down. Adventure fills my soul."
-Captain Santiago Old-Turas

"How did we end up here, Wolf?" asked Old Turas.

"I try not to think about it very much.

"The dream of my reward in Valhalla was taken from me by the Destiny of Tyr and a rogue with a crossbow bolt, so you will forgive me if I seem a bit annoyed about it," said Dragonwülf. All I know now is that we must stop this…Defiler before he destroys the universe. I thought my greatest battles were behind me and I was prepared to lie down, close my eyes, and rest."

"I do not think it is the place of a great warrior to sleep. Sleep is a hiding place, and only *cowards* hide," said Old-Turas.

"The fact that you are almost always right does not take away the fact that I still want to punch you in the face," said Dragonwülf.

"Dreams are for young boys with their lives ahead of them, but sometimes old men like us have our dreams as well. Young men dream of the beautiful girl in the flowery dress and flowing hair while old men dream of the glory days of the fight and the mistakes that altered their lives," said Old Turas.

"He is right, my good man!" said Sir Robert. "I want nothing more now than to demonstrate that I was not dreaming about this voyage and my voyage in eighteen hundred and ninety-four. They said I was an old fool. They will eat their words like a bitter feast."

The mead was passed around to all of the occupants of the ship for all to drink and prepare for the battle of the eternities.

"None for me, mate; I drank enough mead to float the North Hundrun! Rest her old soul," grumbled Old-Turas. "My innards have pretty much spoiled from that rotgut."

"I'll drink your portion then!" yelled Viktor Vorobyev, a new member of Destiny. Viktor had accepted the offer of immortality after being shot by a Memphis, Tennessee, police officer in 1969 AD."I cannot wait for the rumble to start! Are we gonna use chains or clubs, or are we gonna just shoot it out?"

"This might be more of a fight with our wits and cunning rather than blades and hammers," answered Dragonwülf.

"What if we don't have any of those?" asked Luciano Cantore, who had been listening all along. Luciano was an assassinated Chicago low-level Mafia enforcer who had never been accused of possessing an overtly high IQ."I say we just creep on this Defiler mook while he's not lookin' and just whack him."

"It will take much more than that, my good man. The Destiny chaps have told me that the Defiler has been tearing through the universe like the devil himself. He is shrewd and calculating, and we must be that as well," said Sir Robert.

"Let me get close enough to him with my disruptor," said Jarvis Nightwish from the Moon of Saturn. "He will disintegrate like dust in your palms. The Disrupter does not stun; it only destroys."

"It is a good thought, but we must remain poised and ready to strike at any moment like a hungry Rhandobeast," said Dragonwülf.

Avat'or of the Destiny recently resurrected rose to speak. "We will show you the power and the weapons needed to destroy the Defiler. I know what this demon is capable of doing. For this purpose, we have gathered you here."

"We await your wisdom and the wisdom of the Destiny of Tyr," said Dragonwülf.

"The time has not yet come," said Avat'or.

"Damn them and their mysterious *horse manure,*" said Old-Turas under his breath. "At least I am an *honest* pirate."

"We must put this quest in the hands of the gods," said Dragonwülf.

"I thought you had no use for gods and had washed your hands of them?" said Old Turas

"It does not matter how many times I wash my hands; I cannot get the filth to leave my flesh. The gods at least give me hope of peace and some purity to my soul."

"That admission makes you sound weak and not the man of your former days."

"I have seen too much evidence and too many things that prove me wrong. Is that what you wanted to hear, you opinionated bastard? I was wrong. There, I said it," said Dragonwülf.

The Deepwater Watchman was now headed for the Kingdom of Arom to retrieve Queen Valkyrja for the mission at hand.

From the snowy peaks of Arom to the fiery pits of Muspelheim, Queen Valkyrja of the Southlands was hailed as a valiant warrior queen, shield maiden of the gods, and guardian of the Valkyrja. She was famed for her fierce courage and unparalleled battle prowess. The former Valorii Thuireld, the daughter of a peasant woman and King Tin'Old the Second of his name, rose to power as her brother King Tin'Old the Third of his name was murdered by the vicious Hrothgorn of the North.

In the ancient land of Arom, where heroes once roamed and magic filled the air, a prophecy foretold the return of King Draknorr, the dead and defeated King of the Hrothgorn from across space and time. The people of DragonBorne, a bustling town nestled amongst rolling green hills and dotted with sturdy stone buildings, lived in fear of this impending doom.

At the heart of DragonBorne stood the Palace of Stone, a towering castle that served as a powerful symbol of Arom's strength and resilience. Inside the castle's grand halls, a wise and noble ruler named Queen Valkyrja gathered her most trusted advisors to discuss the looming threat.

"My people," the Queen began, her voice filled with authority, "we have received word that Draknorr, ancient and terrible, will soon descend upon our lands once more. We must prepare ourselves for the battle ahead."

A hush fell over the room as the advisors exchanged worried glances. One of them, a grizzled warrior named Svæin, spoke up, his voice rough with concern. "But how can we hope to defeat such a foe that we knew to be dead already? He has already been slain once!"

Valkyrja nodded solemnly. "I know the task before us is daunting, but we cannot afford to cower in fear. We must stand together, united in purpose and resolve, if we are to have any hope of driving him back."

As the advisors debated strategies and tactics late into the night, a lone figure slipped unnoticed into The Palace of Stone's reach. It was a hooded figure, his features obscured in shadow, who approached the throne with a sense of urgency.

"My Queen," the figure whispered, "I bring news that may turn the tide of this coming conflict. I have seen visions of a hero, powerful and brave, who will rise to challenge Draknorr and save us all."

The Queen regarded the hooded figure with a mixture of curiosity and skepticism. "And who is this hero? Do you know their name or their purpose?"

The figure nodded a sense of conviction in their voice. "I know only that they will come from far beyond our world, from a place where time and space are intertwined. They will wield a weapon of great power, forged in the fires of ancient magic, and they will be our salvation."

The advisors listened intently to the figure's words, a glimmer of hope shining in their eyes.

"They?" asked Valkyrja with concern in her voice. "Show me your face, stranger! I must know your countenance at once."

The stranger slowly removed the hood from his head, revealing the hollow stare of empty eye sockets. "I will show the heroes to your throne in one fortnight, Your Majesty. They will rid your kingdom of this scourge," said the stranger.

"Who are you that dare to stand before me with your empty eyes and make just as empty promises?" asked the Queen.

"I am The Harvester of Eyes, known as Hansel Gru'el. I have no eyes."

"I have heard tales of your atrocities. Tell me why I should not take your head from your shoulders now?"

"I am an emissary of one who would come next. I announce the arrival of The Destiny of Tyr and a special passenger whom you know and yet do not know," replied Gru'el.

"Tell me of this mysterious passenger of whom you speak," said the Queen. We were foretold of his arrival by our father Óðinn."

"Destiny has tasked me with keeping this secret until he arrives, Your Majesty. Many apologies, my Queen," said the messenger.

"Depart from me, Harvester! I have no need for a ghoul in my court! Show you to the courtyard and beyond!" ordered the Queen.

"You will require me again, your Grace," said the Harvester as the Queen turned away to address her Knights.

"Oh, my fierce warriors," she began, her silver armor gleaming under the golden light of the hall, "how I long to join you on the battlefield once more, to fight alongside you and feel the thrill of battle coursing through my veins." The Queen's eyes, sharp and filled with determination, now held a hint of excitement as she spoke. "Fate has chosen a direct and bold path for us," she continued, her voice tinged with eagerness. "I must lead you to the front lines and guide you with wisdom and my sword, Kilmister! We will ride out to meet the Hrothgorn and cut them down as fields of wheat!"

Her warriors, clad in shining armor and armed with weapons of divine power, listened intently to their queen's words. They knew the weight of her sacrifice, the burden of leadership that she bore in place of a warrior's life. Yet, they also knew the strength that lay within her, the courage that had led them to victory repeatedly. As Queen Valkyrja looked upon her warriors, her heart swelled with pride and longing.

"Remember, my brave ones," she said, her voice steady and strong once more, "I will fight by your side, and my spirit soars with you on the battlefield. Together, we shall carve our names in the annals of history, a testament to the bond between Queen and warrior."

With a solemn nod, the queen turned to leave the hall, her cape billowing behind her like the wings of a Valkyrja in flight. As she walked away, her warriors stood tall and resolute, ready to face any challenge that came their way, knowing that their queen's spirit would always be with them, guiding them to victory. In that moment, they knew that even in her victory, Queen Valkyrja was the true embodiment of strength, honor, and the people's Queen.

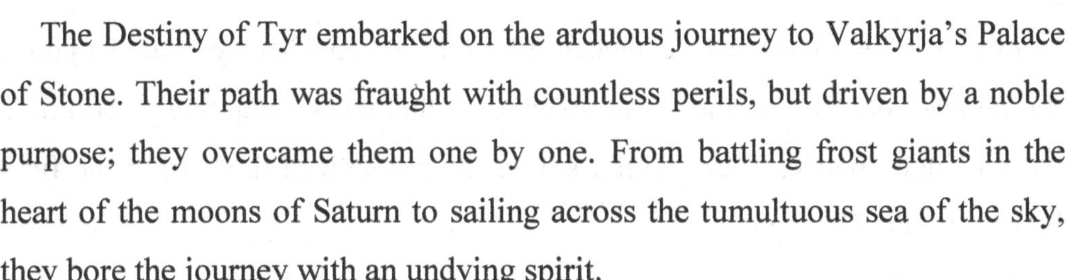

The Destiny of Tyr embarked on the arduous journey to Valkyrja's Palace of Stone. Their path was fraught with countless perils, but driven by a noble purpose; they overcame them one by one. From battling frost giants in the heart of the moons of Saturn to sailing across the tumultuous sea of the sky, they bore the journey with an undying spirit.

As the Destiny of Tyr approached the imposing Palace of Stone, their hearts raced with a mixture of anticipation and apprehension. The gates loomed large before them, a testament to the power and majesty of the good queen Valkyrja, who resided within.

Avat'or, still stinging from his wounds inflicted by the Defiler, raised his sword high and declared, "We have come to seek an audience with Queen Valkyrja. We carry a message of utmost importance that could change the fate of our world!"

The guards at the gate exchanged wary glances before one of them spoke, "Her Majesty is not easily swayed by visitors. What makes you believe you are worthy of her time?"

"You fool! We saved the Kingdom many years ago from the clutches of an evil King named Draknorr. Let us enter!" ordered Avat'or.

The guards conferred briefly before nodding in agreement and opening the gates, allowing the Destiny of Tyr to enter the palace grounds. As they walked through the magnificent halls, adorned with tapestries depicting heroic deeds of old, they were met with whispers and stares from the courtiers and nobles gathered there.

Finally, they stood before Queen Valkyrja, a regal figure seated upon a throne of stone. Her piercing gaze swept over them, assessing their worthiness with a single glance. Then, with a smile, she recognized them from the final battle with the Hrothgorn.

"You will forever be welcome in my realm, my good friends. I owe my life and my kingdom to your bravery," she said, her voice echoing in the grand hall.

Avat'or stepped forward, his voice steady despite the weight of his words. "We come bearing a message of great importance. The balance of the cosmos is in jeopardy, and only you have the power to set things right."

Queen Valkyrja's expression hardened slightly, and she motioned for them to continue.

"Darkness looms on the horizon, threatening to engulf everything in its path," Avat'or added, his voice resonating with urgency. "We need your help to push back this tide of despair and bring light back to our world."

The Queen regarded them thoughtfully for a moment before rising from her throne.

Avat'or, with his imposing presence and glowing blue eyes, knelt before Queen Valkyrja and spoke with a voice that echoed through the throne room. "Mighty Queen, we come to you in our time of need. The Defiler grows stronger with each passing moment, and we require your assistance to vanquish this ancient evil."

Queen Valkyrja, with her fiery red hair and piercing green eyes, regarded Avat'or and his companions with a mix of curiosity and determination. "Tell me more about this Defiler," she commanded, her voice as regal as the mountain winds.

One of the Tyr stepped forward, his eyes filled with sorrow. "Your Majesty, the Defiler is a being of darkness and destruction. It seeks to devour all that is good and pure in the universe, leaving behind nothing but a barren wasteland of despair."

Queen Valkyrja's brow furrowed as she considered the gravity of the situation. "I understand the peril we face," she declared, her voice unwavering. "I will lend you my aid in this noble quest to defeat The Defiler and restore peace to the cosmos."

Avat'or's eyes lit up with gratitude, and he bowed deeply before the Monarch. "Thank you, Queen Valkyrja. Your bravery and kindness will be remembered throughout the ages."

With unwavering resolve, Avat'or and his companions knelt before the regal Queen, their voices ringing out in unison, "We are ready, Your Majesty. Together, we shall overcome whatever stands in our way."

We will return to your Kingdom soon, Your Majesty, and we will bring an old friend with us."

"Is this the one foretold to us by Óðinn?"

"Yes, your Grace, and soon we will see him."

Therefore, the Destiny of Tyr, alongside the good queen Valkyrja, set out once more into the unknown, their bond forged in fire and their destinies intertwined in the eternal struggle between light and darkness.

Artifact Ten

"Hlið valkyrja

ᚺᚾᛁᚾ ᚠᚪᛁᚲᛊᚱᛊᚠ

The Gates of Valkyrja

**Date: Future Dimension of Höðr (2296) CE
Kilometers above the Earth and the Under-Forest)**

"Ek kalla til ríkis míns í nótt, at aldri skuli hræðast meðan ek ber kórónuna.

"I am calling upon my Kingdom tonight to never be afraid as long as I wear the crown."

Some days hence, Queen Valkyrja stood at the grand entrance of the palace of stone, eagerly waiting for the return of her most trusted warrior, Svæin the

Elder. As the gates slowly cracked open, roars of cheers erupted from the palace guards and subjects who had gathered to welcome the hero back from his latest conquest.

"Svæin, you have returned victorious once again!" exclaimed Queen Valkyrja as she stepped forward to congratulate the warrior. "As if I should be surprised whenever you return unscathed from battle!"

"It is my honor to serve you, my Queen," replied Svæin, his voice deep and resonant. "But the true honor is in defending our kingdom and its people."

As they entered the palace, the halls echoed with the sound of their footsteps, a rhythmic beat that symbolized the unity between the warrior and his queen. The walls were adorned with tapestries depicting his brave feats in battle, each thread telling a story of valor and triumph.

"Come, take your place among the brave in my Kingdom. You have earned your place among them," said the Queen. "We are honored you are here."

"It is my duty and my pleasure, my Queen," he replied humbly. "I would lay down my life a thousand times over to ensure the safety of our people."

As they reached the throne room, a lavish feast had been prepared in celebration of the brave man's return. The aroma of roasted meats and spiced wine filled the air, a sensory delight that mirrored the joy and merriment of the gathered guests.

The guests cheered and raised their own goblets in tribute to the warrior, their voices blending in a symphony of gratitude and admiration.

"Your words humble me, my Queen," he said, his voice carrying across the room. "But it is not I who deserves the praise, but all those who stand beside me in defense of our home. Mostly, I wish for the company of our dear departed *Wolfclaw Thur'Gold*."

"Aye," said the Queen. Had we such a man at this time, we would be invincible."

Queen Valkyrja smiled; a rare moment of vulnerability filled her regal features. "We are indeed fortunate to have such a warrior as you. May your strength never waver, and may your sword always be true."

As the night wore on, the celebration continued long into the early hours of the morning, a testament to the unbreakable bond between Queen Valkyrja and her people. In their shared victories and defeats, in their unwavering loyalty and devotion, they stood as a shining example of courage, honor, and love for all who called the Palace of Stone their home.

As the remaining soldiers made their way into the palace, their fellow warriors cheered and clapped, celebrating their return. The halls were adorned with banners and flowers, a tribute to the victorious warriors.

"I bring news from the battlefield, Your Majesty," the leader said, his voice solemn. "Our enemies are gathering their forces, preparing for another attack."

Queen Valkyrja's expression grew grave. "We must be ready for whatever comes our way. Gather the council at once."

As the council convened, the queen and Dragonwülf discussed strategies to defend their kingdom. The tension in the room was palpable, but their determination never wavered.

"We will stand united against our foes," the queen declared, her voice ringing with authority. "Together, we are stronger than any army."

Svaein nodded in agreement. "We will not falter, Your Majesty. We will fight with all our might to protect our land."

The Panorama

Meanwhile, another great council was convening. The Destiny of Tyr returned to the ship, and history was passed in review by the Deepwater Watchman like a panorama of scenes from a cosmic film. They witnessed the Vikings pillaging and burning England, and they saw the fire that started World War I, which was set in Sarajevo, Bosnia, as Santiago Old-Turas gripped the wheel of the Spanish Galion. They watched as the twin titans fell in New York City and the young boy King Tutankhamun was gently carried into his tomb. All the while, the Deepwater Watchman carried a gallery of assassins, warriors, and murderers.

The caretakers, The Destiny of Tyr, watched intently as their ship cut through time and space on the way to an appointment with history. The Ice Giants killed and destroyed the civilization of the Saturn Moon Enceladus

Colony, while a lost Prince Tin'Old found his way back to the palace in the time of DragonBorne. Time drifted by, and each of the passengers was released by the Destiny to their respective dimensions to be called upon later. The Panorama received the passengers of the Deepwater Watchman and the unfinished stories of their lives.

"Am I returning to the Kingdom to serve my Queen?" asked Dragonwülf. My shipmates are returning to their worlds. What is the purpose of assembling our fellowship to dissolve it? It is madness."

Avat'or of the Destiny was quick with his answer.

"They will be called upon as we need them. We need you now. The world needs you at present. We have traveled to see Queen Valkyrja."

"Queen Valorii is her name…not Valkyrja," Dragonwülf replied with indignation.

"We whispered in the ear of her mother at the time of the Queen's birth her precise name, but she did not understand, and Valorii was the result. She has wings! How could you not have known she was a Valkyrja?" answered Avat'or.

Unknown to the crew of the ship, evil was descending upon the kingdom of Arom and Queen Valkyrja. The Hrothgorn were approaching from the Northlands.

The Queen sat uneasily on her throne.

"I am uncomfortable with the wings. They keep me from moving the way I choose. They are also heavy," complained the Queen. "They make me feel like a prisoner rather than a Queen of the realm.

"How am I supposed to do battle with an enemy with so much weight on my back?" she complained." I am a warrior, not a flying princess!"

"Your majesty looks so lovely in the wings that the entire kingdom is envious of you," reasoned a lady in waiting.

"Do not envy feathers. Envy my skill in battle. Envy my honor and my willingness to give myself for my kingdom," the Queen retorted. "Feathers are for chickens and ducks."

Apparently, the novelty of wings had grown tiresome for some time.

Upon arriving at Valkyrja's grand hall, The Destiny marveled at the soaring, regal architecture, embellished with intricate patterns of ancient battles. Valkyrja, swathed in her battle gear, greeted Tyr with an aura of respect and strength.

The Destiny of Tyr appeared at the throne room door. Each one is adorned with robes and the symbols of the stars upon them.

"We must introduce you to someone near to your heart."

Out of the shadows, surrounded by the Destiny of Tyr, appeared *Dragonwülf*. The Queen's eyes met the old warrior's eyes and locked their gaze upon him.

"Your majesty, we present to you one known as Dragonwülf."

The sight of an old friend shocked her. "This cannot be," said the queen in a wavering voice. "You look like Wolfclaw… but it cannot be."

"I assure you, it is me."

"Wolfclaw… you are the one they call Dragonwülf?

"I am the one known as Dragonwülf.

The Queen embraced her old friend and held him tightly.

"I thought you were dead and gone to Valhalla? I do not understand."

It warms my heart to see you. We must ask your friends to be present," said the Queen.

"I am sorry, majesty; there is no time for reunions. I have been told that this evil one they describe has killed the peacemakers of history, and he must be stopped."

This puzzled the Queen. "What do the peacemakers have to do with this Kingdom?"

"History has killed all of them; all those we call dreamers and creators have been brought low. No new songs or visions will be given. They have spat in the eyes of the gods! We must fight to make sure that does not happen again by stopping the one who would alter history and destroy peace. Come with us and save the world again, Your Majesty!" said Dragonwülf as he sank to one knee in respect to the queen.

"I could never say no to you, my old friend, but we must protect our kingdom at all costs," reminded the Queen. "Arise. I am not worthy of that kind of worship. I can feel the spirit of the pounding march of the Hrothgorn approaching Arom. We will be at the ready and *hack* their leathery necks with our swords as soon as they approach. Then we will hunt for The Defiler. I am forever at your Service, but we must defeat the Hrothgorn first."

"Thank you, my Queen. I must return to the Deepwater; we have much to do. Call upon me if you need help, and I will come to you," said Dragonwülf.

"I know very few things to be true in this world of folly and lies, but I know you, my friend. I know you can be counted upon to have honor and fellowship with me, and you have never broken those bonds!" said the Queen.

"My path has been strewn with sacrifices, but I have never wavered, for in the end, it is not the accolades that define a man, but the commitments to a code of honor that guides me. I may not always emerge victorious, but I will always fight with honor and dignity," said Dragonwülf.

The Queen reached out to her old friend and embraced him. "Peace and victory shall be yours and …be safe, my friend."

"I am always yours until I return to my Queen."

Artifact Eleven

Steel, Blood and Bone

Dimension of Loki 1969 AD- Earth

"I left those demons of Hell behind in flames as they breathed the fumes of my celestial bike!"
Viktor Vorobyev.

The Deepwater Watchman flew into the ever-changing channels of the universal corridors of time and deposited Biker Viktor Vorobyev into late 20th-century Earth.

Under the watchful eye of Avat'or and the Destiny of Tyr, in another scene from the celestial panorama, Viktor walked into his friend's house. His friend Jake was a fellow biker with a charming smile and a beautiful wife. The jovial atmosphere quickly soured as tensions rose between them. Words turned to intense arguments, and before he knew it, he found himself gripping a bottle of his friend's pride whiskey, the amber liquid sloshing uneasily inside. The room felt suffocating, the air thick with unspoken accusations and simmering anger.

"I can't believe you'd do this to me," his friend's voice rose, his face contorted in betrayal. "You did this in my own house! You're supposed to be my brother!"

Viktor took a long swig from the bottle, the burn of the alcohol offering a fleeting distraction from the mess of emotions swirling inside him.

I can't believe you would get your boxers in a big wad over some crappy whiskey!" said Viktor to his friend.

"You fool; you think this is about whiskey? You really think that?"

"What's it about then?" asked Viktor, even though he really knew.

It's about Astrid, you moron!" his friend bellowed.

"Maybe if you paid more attention to her, I wouldn't have to," Viktor retorted, his words laced with superiority.

The friend's eyes narrowed, and a dangerous stare flashed across them. "She's off-limits, and *you know it*. You've crossed a line, man." Jake threw a left hook and connected with Viktor's chin, knocking him from his feet.

"If ya get up, I'm gonna knock you clean out, Vik! You touch my lady again, I'll kill ya!" swore Jake.

Before he could respond, sudden darkness enveloped Viktor's vision, and the world slipped away as if swallowed by a black hole. Panic surged through him as he fought against the void, struggling to make sense of what was happening. In the darkness, a haunting refrain echoed through his mind. He stumbled to his feet, reached for his boot dagger, and produced a flash, a glint of steel, and then a scream. Astrid ran from the bedroom upon hearing Jake scream and then blackness.

Did I kill somebody? Did I just kill Jake?

The words echoed ominously, a chilling reminder of the chaos that had unfolded. His heart raced, the weight of guilt settling heavily on my shoulders. There would be no clues and no remnants of what had transpired if he took his dagger with him. He could hear the questions of police detectives. What would they ask the next day? He wondered if Astrid would inform the police about him.

No, she would not do that!

Veins pulsed in his eardrums, a relentless drumbeat that matched the racing of his heart. Each throb felt like an accusation, a reminder of the irreversible actions that had led to this moment of reckoning. The world seemed to blur around him, reality fracturing as he grappled with the uncertainty of what lay beyond the blackness that had consumed him.

What is the banging at the door?

The words reverberated through his mind, a cacophony of sound that drowned out all other thoughts. Panic clawed at Viktor's chest, a primal fear that threatened to overwhelm him. He stumbled forward, each step taking him closer to the edge of sanity as he wrestled with the possibility of what he had done. The image of Astrid flashed before his eyes, her screaming ringing in his ears. He loved her with a passion. He could never tell Jake, and he never would. He wanted her more than he could ever say. He often thought he would kill Jake and run away with Astrid, but he knew she never would.

He even ran the idea by her once or twice. She told him long ago, "You are a love-struck boy making the entire world sad with your terrible sad songs. Grow up."

He answered her, "I love you so much I would gladly rot in a prison of my own making. I would just kiss you through the bars on visiting days and be happy forever."

"You are a fool, and you'd better not do what you are thinking about....I mean it," she answered.

Now he had done it for real.

Guilt and desire waged war within him, a tangled mess of emotions that threatened to consume him whole. He reached out a trembling hand, grasping at the fleeting memories of a life that now seemed like a distant dream.

In the darkness, a single question lingered, a haunting reminder of the truth that he could no longer escape.

Viktor knew he had killed Jake. Did the Destiny of Tyr think he could undo one of the many murders he had committed? He stumbled outside, fired up his bike, and headed out into the night, roaring against the darkness.

A cold chill traveled down Viktor's back. He was back on his bike again, and he recognized *this* night. It was more than just a bad case of Déjà vu. He had been here before. He had already lived that night. That night…this same night, a cop blew Viktor's head off in the ravine not too far from this location. Destiny and Dragonwülf should have released him a day earlier or a day later.

Dragonwülf and the crew of the Deepwater dropped him into this time spectrum for a reason. They told him it was to regain balance in the universe. He promised Viktor he would be able to reconcile his timeline.

They put me right back here to relive this all over.
He's gonna make me get my head blown off again.
Lying' piece of Viking trash. He probably thinks it is funny.

Viktor had no choice in the matter. It was the agreement he made with The Destiny of Tyr to let him live as an immortal. He had an appointment with Officer Johnson of the Tennessee Highway Patrol. He would die at the hands of the Officer, as in the original record of The Destiny of Tyr.

The highway took a ribbon-turn away from the tracks, and once again, he was on his own. He rode on until the night became dusky dawn. A speeding

Buick grazed Viktor's hip as it went by. It almost threw the whole bike off the road.

"This hog ain't no go-kart," he said in a loud booming voice.

It could be that he was daydreaming about Astrid instead of noticing what was behind him on the road. He was looking for the horses that belonged to the Destiny of Tyr from the last time he was here. *This is different.* The sound startled him as he heard the roar of five huge Rat-Bikes that overtook him. Rat bikes were motorcycles that were held together by car parts, welding, and just plain luck. The pipes were louder than Viktor had ever heard.

I can't say anything about these guys trying to keep their bikes together, even if they do look like dumpster fires.

The riders were flying red and black, almost like a flag without the stars. These boys were patched, too. They passed Viktor on both sides and left him in the middle of the formation. The heavy motorcycles slowed to a stop on an access road. Viktor was curious about the leader of the crew, who was an older, gray Hispanic man. He was covered in leather, complete with motorcycle chaps. This was no *weekender*. He thought better of stopping, but curiosity overwhelmed him.

"What's your story?" the big old rider asked.

"Story?" asked Viktor incredulously. I ain't got a freakin' story. You guys stopped me! I ride with Maniacs MC. Who are you with?"

"Locos Muertos!" the old biker bellowed, pumping his fist in triumph with the other four men as if in celebration. "I'm Mongrel, and these four guys are just a pain in my ass."

"That's not even your name," one of the other men said. "Your real name is Hector."

"Keep talking smart, man, I could still beat you even with my bad knees, so don't mess with me," he said, leaning in and raising his voice.

The younger biker cowered in fear, knowing the older man could do as he promised.

Hector turned his attention to Viktor. "Look, man, we just wanted to let you know that we lost two Locos on this stretch between Little Rock and Memphis."

"Lost 'em how? Did they beef it on the highway?" asked Viktor.

"No dude, they just… disappeared. Just be careful. They never made it to Memphis, so we are out looking for them. Los Lobos lost three of their dudes here about ten days ago, the same way. Cops did nothin', they never found their bikes or nothin'," said Hector.

"Where are you headed?" asked Viktor.

"We got a date with the universe, I guess you could say," answered Hector.

"I don't get that. What are you talkin' about?"

"It's time to even things up, *homes*."

Viktor remained silent and stared at his feet.

They have to be part of The Destiny of Tyr because nobody else talks like this.

"We gotta go, man. Keep going and *don't stop,* and we'll see you on the other side," said Hector.

"The other side of what?" asked Viktor.

The bikers awkwardly stared at one another and waited for words that were not to come.

Los Muertos roared to life again and disappeared into the dawn without an answer.

Viktor swallowed a lump and felt that familiar flutter in his gut.

I can't believe I am going to have to do this all over again. I never heard of the Muertos, but they looked scared.

Viktor had a case of monkey butt from the long ride and was in a bad mood. He saw the lights of a roach motel ahead. He knew he needed some sleep, and this place looked cheap enough. He pushed on instead.

The next day, somewhere on the vast expanse of Interstate 40 out in the middle of the state, he came to the hairpin curve off a side road that he took to get fuel. The Phillips station was the only thing on this exit. He almost did not clear it at the speed at which he was traveling. He took the turn and instantly knew something was wrong. He turned his bike around and went back. There in the ravine, almost not visible from the road, were the remains of several mangled motorcycles. He could see they were the Rat-bikes from yesterday.

He got off his bike and went into the ravine with a flashlight. He saw Muertos Loco's jackets strewn all over the area.

Oh my God, what in the hell happened here?

There were twisted and mangled bodies everywhere. The level of savagery done to these bodies could not have happened from a simple accident. They looked as if they had been murdered by some kind of animal. Some of the Locos were not intact. Some were even missing their heads. Viktor considered calling the police, but he knew that was a bad idea.

I got too many warrants and I ain't going back to jail. Besides, it will not take the law too long to find a big pile of bodies out here.

Viktor rode on for another twenty miles. He started to feel bad about just leaving those guys out there in the sticks for the birds to pick on. *All of a sudden, I got a conscience.* He thought as he turned around and went back. He saw the Phillips station and went to the ravine. A huge hole was there in the place where the mangled bodies and motorcycles had been. A chill ran down Viktor's spine as he peered into the gaping dark hole where Muertos had died. As he tried to make some sense of the scene, a flashlight threw a beam over his shoulder into the hole.

That fateful night, a harrowing sight would forever etch itself in Viktor's mind: the disjointed rhythm of bullets piercing the night air, cries swallowed by the roaring winds, and the crumbling of man's beloved domain. Amidst the chaos, he turned to look but found himself face to face with a barrel cold and impersonal. A crack split the night, and in a flash. Officer Johnson's steely stare seared his eyes. A bullet pierced his forehead all the way to the back of his head with a splitting pain reminiscent of an ax in the skull. Viktor pierced the veil of time itself—his fate forever altered by a murky past.

Then, reality *shifted* like an otherworldly veil. Viktor found himself back in the same roadside ravine, where moonlight dances over stained asphalt. Above him were the crumbling remnants of MC Los Muertos, but this time he witnessed their fall without a bullet lodged in his skull. He had cheated death in the blink of an eye. There was no Officer Johnson, and his head remained intact. As he peered into the dark chasm, he could hear the roaring of waves beating on the shores of an ocean. He could see the breakers and the black sea beneath. He remembered his rebirth in a similar body of water in his previous timeline.

Frozen in disbelief, he trod the familiar territory and attempted to protect himself against what he remembered. Viktor scanned the horizon for the cop, the forerunner of his abrupt end in what was the old timeline.

A sudden shriek stole away his relief.

The field was a rain of human despair, cascading down into a gaping chasm that led to the fathomless heart of the ocean.

The leaders of two motorcycle gangs sat atop the knoll on their bikes. The Destiny of Tyr watched from the hilltop.

"Vorobyev has done well, Avat'or," said one of the council.

"We will see what comes," said the wise leader.

Viktor was about to witness the unthinkable.

Artifact Twelve

Celestial Rumble

Dimension of Loki 1969 CE- Earth

"The universe can go to hell. I'm done and I ain't doing this anymore!"

Tonight we show the world that we will not be what they want us to be," said the first leader of a large motorcycle club, a big man called Big Mike. *"This is it, man."* Actually, it was a gang, but it sounded more reputable to call it a club.

"Damn straight. I would rather go down fighting with my brothers than end up in a freakin' nursing home. Just shoot me instead. That ain't any way to live," said his counterpart, Pete.

"Okay, you hoist your colors, and I hoist mine…it's time," said Big Mike.

Both men put red and black colors on the handlebars of their machines.

"Let's get down, brother," said Pete as he reached across the bikes and shook his friend's hand.

"It was a helluva ride, man," said Mike.

"Meet me on the other side, my friend. I will wait on the shore for you."

In the face of a horrific spectacle, each side splashed a death knell—a symphony of the ghastly orchestrated by fate. Viktor felt powerless as the combatants plunged into the depths of the ocean beneath the ravine one by one. Yet, Viktor was not a mere onlooker in this timeline; he was an unwilling actor caught in a dreadful spectacle in the theater of the absurd.

Fueled by desperation, he sprinted away from the chasm. He looked back into the abyss, only to be greeted by the eerie tranquility of oblivion. It was the ocean hundreds of meters below him. Viktor felt the weight of The Destiny of Tyr pushing him onto his knees. He was being swallowed by the ocean's unseen depths. How could he defeat the grisly jaws of mortality only to fall into another cruel trap? He was being swallowed up by the combat of the two motorcycle gangs fighting to the death. His heartbeat seemed to echo across the dread-filled streets of this tiny town just off the exit from Interstate 40 as the reality of the fate he had outrun crashed down on him. Tonight, they would sacrifice themselves in honor of the lives they had lived.

That night, a few blocks away, the cop who had previously killed him wandered, unaware of his night's gory existence in another timeline. The timeline splintered once again, the cop and his bullet fell off course, oblivious to the tragedy and grief that had woven itself into Viktor's identity. The cop was now innocently writing a speeding ticket.

In Vorobyev's world, he was not silenced by the grim reaper's bullet but by the ocean's insatiable maw. Bitter regret hung heavy in the air. Could fate be so ruthless as to carve an even crueler destiny than the former one he suffered?

Underneath a Tennessee moon's cold glow, an event arose that reshaped history. As the night blanket covered the ground, there, one hundred bikers cast their last full measure of devotion and honor into the fire of a dying brotherhood.

They were warriors; their horsepower was parallel to the stars. They struggled to keep honor's knot fastened tight amidst stinging cinders and biting chill, their unblemished valor dripping from each studded gear, each worked leather, each organic scar, as they prepared to ride into the stained horizon of a last crusade. Swearing upon their life, they vowed to give their all, reflecting on the way they had lived. The traditional colors were hoisted, and the ensuing melee ensued. They were like moths drawn to a flame, their bodies and bikes moving as one.

The combat was homage to their way of life. It was too late for Viktor to retreat. He was caught in the middle of the melee with no escape. The massive motorcycles lined up, roaring on opposite ends of the field. The engines raced in a terrifying show of unrelenting power. The sound of a hundred clutches engaging filled the air with a clap of thunder as the steel horses charged straight at one another. The smashing of steel, aluminum, and rubber sent an overwhelming roar into the sky, blocking out the screams of the dying men.

Amidst a crescendo of revving engines, the battle erupted. The night was soon illuminated by exploding Molotov cocktails, leaving behind trails of fire. The sounds of metal clashing against metal were accompanied by screams of fury from both sides. It was a rock concert of chaos and fury, thrilling and terrifying simultaneously.

The scene turned into a confusing maze of metal, smoke, and screeching tires. Every rider was engaged in a deadly dance, their fists flying, chains whirling, and blood spilling.

Punches flew, kicks landed, and motorcycles collided, creating a symphony of destruction. The battleground became a swirling vortex of pain, anger, and adrenaline. Booted feet stomped upon the pavement, leaving scars that marked the territory of this brutal confrontation.

Despite the bloodshed, a sense of honor lingered among the chaos. It was a battle for supremacy, a fight to protect the pride and loyalty of their respective gangs. The warriors, battered and bruised, fought with unwavering determination, their comrades always by their side.

Amidst the chaos, the leaders finally locked eyes. Big Mike and Pete, their faces etched with battle scars, charged toward each other. Time seemed to halt as they collided with the force of a thousand raging storms. The clash of their fists echoed through the night, sparks flying from the contact.

Blade, swift and nimble, evaded Pete's bone-crushing blows, retaliating with precise strikes. Mike, fueled by brute strength, attempted to overpower Pete, his strikes thunderous and relentless. The two leaders fought with a deadly fluidity, their determination paving the way for a final showdown.

The streets bore witness to an epic battle that shook the very foundations of the city. The fate of these two deadly motorcycle gangs hung in the balance, their legacies forged in the fires of this violent confrontation.

When the dust finally settled, only the legacy of bloodshed remained. Both brave biker gangs lie dead on the field, only moments later to be swept into the abyss and down to the underworld and the undersea. Closing his eyes, Viktor took a deep breath and let go of the anger and fear that had fueled his life. In that moment of surrender, he found a strength he had never known before.

As the dust settled and the echoes of battle faded into the night, Viktor stood victorious, his heart pounding with a mixture of exhaustion and triumph. His universe had been restored to harmony, and Viktor had found redemption in the most unlikely of places - on the back of his bike, surrounded by enemies and strangers.

With a final glance at the stars above, Viktor revved his engine once more and surveyed all that was before him. There were no more gangs. There were no bodies, just a tangled mess of steel, and the smell of gas and oil in the air.

Viktor peered into the massive hole before him and listened carefully. He heard the screams of the tortured and the tormented souls. Suddenly, he heard a sound behind him, a snapping dry twig, but in the silence, it was deafening.

"You must go!" The voice behind him said, as Viktor spun around to face the figure, it was the ghostly form of his friend Jake.

"Jake! How in the hell… where did you… I don't…" Viktor could form no words.

"Shut the hell up! You murdered me when I was not on my game! There's no way you would have gotten over on me otherwise, you sneaky bastard," said Jake.

"You know I was drunk, man…"

"It doesn't matter. That is not why I am here. Listen to me! Right after I lay there bleeding out, a demon appeared to me and told me that he had dragged Astrid to Hell at the order of some dude he called The Defiler. He made me repeat it; that is how I remember it. This defiler dude hates you for some reason. Do you know who he is?" asked Jake.

" Yeah, I think I might."

"He says you gotta go get her if you want her. He sounds like he wants you more than he wants Astrid. Get her! Save her!" said Jake as his form and last words faded into eternity and dispersed like smoke.

The gaping hole in front of him beckoned. It made sense now that he should ride into the wide-open maw of the earth. For some reason, it called to him. He knew the screams from beneath, including Astrid's screams.

Viktor revved his motorcycle as he smelled the breeze that was permeated with gasoline and death as he raced toward the edge of the abyss. There was no other way to get there. This had to be the portal to Hell. Without hesitation, he accelerated and soared off the jagged rocks, his heart pounding in exhilaration as he plummeted into the dark abyss below. The bike and Viktor fell for what seemed to be hours. The bike landed with a spine-numbing crash in the red-hot coals below. Strangely enough, it landed upright with its rider still in the saddle.

In the depths of the underworld, where the flames danced hungrily and the shadows whispered wicked secrets, Viktor Vorobyev revved up his motorcycle. The hum of the engine seemed to clash with the eerie silence that enveloped him as he gazed ahead at the towering gates of Hell.

With a fierce nod, Viktor gunned the engine and charged forward, the gates of Hell parting before him with an ominous creak. The motorcycle tore through the gate opening and threw coals behind it. The demons that guarded the gate were caught unaware, as they had not expected to see a motorcycle. The air grew thick with the scent of sulfur as he raced deeper into the realm of darkness, his only guiding light the fiery glow emanating from his bike.

As he rode, the ground trembled beneath him, and a figure appeared in their path, blocking their way. Ar'goros, a demon with twisted horns and eyes that glowed like embers, sneered at him malevolently.

"Ah, Viktor Vorobyev, you dare to enter the domain of The Defiler? We knew you would come. There is something reliable about those who are part of the Destiny of Tyr," Ar'goros hissed.

"The Destiny of what? I never heard of 'em," said Viktor.

You lie! You have no honor," said Ar'goros.

"I am in hell. I thought anything goes down here," Viktor taunted.

"Enjoy your jest, you fool! You will never leave this place, especially not with your precious woman," the demon said as he held Astrid in his claws as she struggled to escape. She began to scream in pain while writhing to escape his clutches.

"If you hurt her, there is no place you can ever hide from me," Viktor said. "I don't care if you are a demon or a god, I will kill you."

"That is some grand talk from someone in your position," said the demon. You cannot bargain with me."

Viktor clenched his jaw, his grip on the handlebars tightening. "I will not let you or your masters keep her from me. Stand aside!"

With a roar, Ar'goros lunged forward, his claws slashing through the air. Viktor swerved to avoid the attack, his motorcycle skidding dangerously close to the edge of another yawning chasm. He reached into his leather, pulled a large dagger from his pant leg, and dismounted his bike.

Ar'goros threw Astrid to the ground behind him. "Watch how a real man fights a weak and tiny boy-man. You will be mine first before I bring you to the defiler."

"No, I will never belong to anyone! You are going to have to kill me first, but I will never give myself to you, *spawn of Hades*!" said Astrid. "You're messing with the wrong person," she bellowed.

As the clash of steel and fury echoed through the infernal landscape, Viktor and Ar'goros fought with all their might, good and evil entwined in a dance of death. Sparks flew as the blade met claws, and the ground shook with the force of their combat.

"You have no idea the forces that you have awoken!" Ar'goros bellowed, his voice echoing in the cavernous depths. "We are the bringers of despair, the tormentors of souls! Destiny does not care for you, or they would be here!"

Viktor, fueled by love and determination, pressed on. His courage was unwavering in the face of darkness. With a final, decisive blow, he plunged his long dagger into the face of the screaming Ar'goros and overpowered him, sending him tumbling into the abyss with a deafening roar and shriek as he fell into the endless Abyss.

"Good one, Vik!" said Astrid. She smiled, her gaze filled with gratitude and love. "I was not sure if you would come for me. I thought I was just an afterthought to you. I could have killed him myself, though. I was just waiting for you…you know, just to make you feel better."

Viktor gave her a side glance. "Get on… let's get the hell out of here."

Astrid held tight and whispered in his ear. "I see what you did there. That was pretty funny."

Viktor Vorobyev revved his motorcycle engine, the sound echoing through the fiery pits of hell. He turned to Astrid, clutching him tightly. "Hold on tight, baby," he called over the roaring flames. "We're getting out of here."

Astrid tightened her grip around Viktor, fear and determination written across her face.

As they sped through the twisting, fiery roads of hell, they encountered all manner of monstrous creatures and obstacles trying to stop them. "We can do this!" Viktor shouted, swerving past a horde of demons.

Astrid nodded, her eyes scanning their surroundings. "Viktor, look out!" she screamed as a flaming boulder came hurtling towards them.

Viktor expertly maneuvered the motorcycle, narrowly avoiding the boulder. "Good eye," he said with a grin.

After what seemed like an eternity of dodging and weaving through the treacherous terrain, they finally reached the gates of hell. Standing in their way was the gatekeeper, a towering figure with flaming eyes and a sword of pure fire.

"No one ever goes *this* way," the gatekeeper boomed, blocking their path.

"Neither one of us belongs here in this hotel hell, and it's check-out time!" said Viktor.

Viktor glanced at Astrid, determination etched on his face. "We've come too far to be stopped now," he declared. "Hold on, we're going through."

With a defiant roar, Viktor opened the throttle and sped toward the gatekeeper. Astrid closed her eyes, expecting the worst. "Maybe next time I drive, is that okay with you?" she asked.

At the last moment, Viktor veered sharply to the side, narrowly missing the gatekeeper and crashing through the gates of hell. As they burst through the fiery barrier, a blinding light enveloped them, and they found themselves hurtling towards the surface.

The next thing they knew, Viktor and Astrid were lying on the soft grass, the sun shining down on them. They had escaped hell together, their love and determination guiding them through the darkest of trials.

Viktor turned to Astrid, a wide grin on his face. "We made it, Astrid. We're finally free."

Astrid smiled back at him, relief and love shining in her eyes. "I wouldn't have gotten out without you, Viktor. I love you," she said as Viktor became surrounded by blackness and swirling, spinning confusion. He found himself spinning and turning in the water.

"I love you, too!" he screamed as he faded away. He looked but could not find her.

His world became dark as he sank to the bottom of the sea and sucked the murky seawater into his heaving lungs.

Just as Viktor had resolved to give in to the sea's death, he felt a large, burly arm reach down and grab him by his leather jacket.

A waterlogged and drowned Viktor looked up from the deck to see the image of Dragonwülf, his weathered face marked with scars of battles long past.

Dammit! Why couldn't you just wait a couple of minutes so I could talk to Astrid?" yelled Viktor.

"Do you want me to return you to the water?

"No, but your timing was really bad, the worst ever. That's the story of my life," said Viktor.

The old Norseman took a deep breath before speaking.

"Come with me. Death will not come to you yet. We have much work to do," he said as the two were pulled aboard the Deepwater.

"I fixed everything. I did what you sent me to do. Ain't I done?" asked Viktor. "Where is Astrid? Is she dead?

"No brave one, she has been returned to her timeline and is quite safe. Viktor was overcome, as once again, true love escaped him.

"It was cruel to give her to me and then take her away. I should punch you in the mouth for that," he threatened.

"You are needed by the universe for so much more than that," said Dragonwülf.

"The universe can go to hell. I'm done and I ain't doing this anymore!"

"Aye, young warrior, balance in the universe is like the dance of the gods and the giants. So no, my friend, you are not done, he said in jest, mocking Viktor's language."

"What are you talking about? I'm not that smart, but the least you could do is dumb it down for me!" said Viktor with a raised voice.

Dragonwülf continued, his voice carrying the weight of ancient wisdom. "In my world, we see balance in the eternal struggle between order and chaos, light and darkness, creation and destruction. It is in the clash of opposites that the universe finds a way to balance. There will be time for love upon another day."

Viktor nodded, his expression thoughtful. "I guess I get it. I have always seen balance in the way my motorcycle glides through the winding roads. I feel like I am one with the machine. Is that what you are talking about?"

Dragonwülf smiled, his eyes twinkling with recognition. "Aye, young steel horse rider, the balance you find in your journey is but a reflection that controls all things.

"Welcome back into our fellowship, Viktor," said Dragonwülf. "You have reconciled your universe."

"What about Jake? I killed my friend. I can't undo that," said a dejected Viktor

"Jake will continue in his death," answered Dragonwülf.

"I don't get it."

"In the flames of anger, you lost yourself. But justice has been served," said Dragonwülf. "Jake was cruel and vicious to Astrid. He injured her many times in her mind and body. You served a feast of justice for him. Let him eat his fill. The universe is better for it."

Artifact Thirteen

Áss sverða

ᚠᛖᛖ ᛖᛈᛗᚱᛈᚠ

The Ace of Swords

Dimension of Óðinn 140 CE

Underforest Lands Kingdom of Arom

"You run through me, and I cannot escape your grasp.
You are a vicious vampire to my soul!"

Some days hence, at dawn, as the sun rose like a lazy emperor from a
weekend sleep, the impending attack was building from the North. The sound
of automatic gunfire in the distance awakened the Kingdom of Arom from its
lazy slumber. The rat-a-tat-tat-tat of the machine guns rebounded from the
walls of the kingdom. They were approaching. The heavy marching of the

enormous beasts shook the earth beneath as the Hrothgorn trudged a straight line to the Kingdom of Arom.

"March on, you filthy slime!" barked the General of the ranks of the Hrothgorn guard. "We must breach the walls of the kingdom. Therein lies our King."

The gate to the kingdom of Arom lay before the Hrothgorn army like a monstrous stone mound. It was even taller than a Hrothgorn. Each Hrothgorn guard held a mechanical crossbow. They were adorned with golden details. There were also golden spikes protruding from the top of the entrance. As the Hrothgorn troops marched to the kingdom, a golden horn sliced through the billowing dust clouds of the rear guard. It blew for the third time, and the entire Arom army came out into the light. Three blaring blasts and a golden roar ripped through the air. The Arom army had arrived. These troops wore helmets of deer horn, and their skin looked as if silver had been poured into their pores.

The squealing of the tracks from the tanks all but drowned the harsh voice of General Kor.

"Find Queen Valkyrja and bring her to me! There is a seat in the palace for the Hroth soldier who brings me the Queen alive."

"We will do as you command, oh great one!" said a Hroth soldier, bowing as he spoke.

"Be silent, fool, and do my will. Your flattery will put you in the stewpot by the end of the day," threatened Kor. "We will storm the gates of Arom and take what is ours to take. We will steal the spoils of war to pay for our new palace. Take the women for ourselves and kill everyone else. These are orders. They are not open to negotiation. These peasants burnt our palace to the ground, and now we will litter that same ground with their burnt corpses."

The Hrothgorn army had changed its uniforms since the days of the fellowship of Wolfclaw. They wore gleaming armor forged of shining steel. They carried automatic weapons, side arms, and broad swords for close combat. General Kor had visited the portal of the pines with the Witch Queen to procure unusual weapons. The formidable sight approaching the kingdom was enough to cause a freezing sweat to roll down the back of even the most seasoned warrior.

In the palace, Queen Valkyrja had been planning for the invasion of the Hrothgorn.

"We will stand and fight these agents of evil until there is not one left standing!" ordered the Queen. "All able-bodied people follow Dragonwülf to the gates. Ser Kilmister and I will join soon."

Two brothers who were Hrothgorn soldiers approached the gate of the city of Arom. In the ranks of the Hrothgorn, there was dissension and murmurings.

"How long must we march and die for this old fool?" asked a young Hroth soldier.

"You mean Kor?" asked another.

"Yes. Surely you do not think we could capture the Queen from the kingdom of Arom?" the young soldier asked." King Draknorr was our King, but now he is dead, killed by the sword of the Queen. I saw his corpse. He is dead. He was stabbed through the heart. He is dead. Why do you not understand that? Kor means to march us all to our deaths to avenge a dead King. He will still be dead!"

"Keep your voice down, you fool! Do you mean for us to be overheard? You are right. This is a fool's errand. Draknorr does not live except in the mind of Kor. We are to approach and guard the gates of the city. No one comes in or out, it is the decree of General Kor," said Cen' Tar, the senior officer. "Do you hear me?"

"You never pull rank on me when we are in front of other soldiers. Why are you doing it now that we are alone?" asked Orgoth, the younger soldier. "I thought you and I would die together in battle if needed. I hate that making war keeps us at arm's length. I hate war completely. I am done with Kor.

"You know what I mean! Stop trying to make it seem like I think you are somehow lesser than me," said Cen' Tar. "I trust you to keep me safe while we march to do things we would rather not do."

"I cannot do this anymore," said Orgoth with a shaking voice. We are supposed to be bloodthirsty and ruthless, but I do not feel that way. I can no longer kill."

"We have been defeated in war and cut into pieces. We marched until our feet were bleeding. Kor sits in his tank and orders us to die for Hrothgorn," said Cen'Tar in final agreement.

"I will never go to someone's golden shore again just to kill them… my weapon is an ornament only," said Orgoth, throwing his sword to the ground. Orgoth reached to embrace Cen'Tar, who pulled away sharply.

"Wait until we cannot be seen, you fool! Are you trying to get us killed?" asked an agitated Cen'Tar. "Stay away from the damned walls and cover-up. No one can see us embrace. You know it will make us look weak!"

"This will not do. I am no longer full of vengeance and hate. I am not afraid."

"That is easy for you to say!" snapped Cen'Tar, gathering his thoughts…I know…you are right. We must find a way to escape this."

Alongside you, I have survived in a relentless world of pain and hate," said Orgoth.

Cen'Tar threw his sword and hammer to the ground, and together they ran into the forest forever, leaving the Hrothgorn way of life. The story of Cen'Tar and Orgoth is still being written in the panorama of time.

Queen Valkyrja bore an astonishing possession: a talking sword named Kilmister. This was no ordinary weapon; it held the soul of a former enslaved person who, in his mortal form, used to serve the Hrothgorn. Forged centuries ago, Kilmister had since existed as a sentient blade, trapped and detached from the intimate sensations of humanity he yearned for.

In the grand throne room of the kingdom of Arom, Queen Valkyrja stood proudly clad in her regal armor, a majestic sword at her side.

"Ser Kilmister, my faithful companion," Queen Valkyrja spoke softly, her voice resonating with authority and respect. "What news do you bring to me today?"

The sword's blade shimmered as it replied in a deep, resonant voice, "My Queen, there are whispers of unrest in the Kingdom. The dark forces are stirring once more, and they threaten to bring chaos upon our lands."

Valkyrja's brow furrowed at the news, a flash of concern crossing her royal features. "We cannot allow this darkness to spread," she declared firmly. "Prepare our troops for battle, Ser Kilmister. We shall ride out at dawn to confront this threat head-on."

The sentient sword hummed in agreement, its blade glowing with determination. "As you command, my Queen. We shall stand together against the shadows that seek to engulf us."

Queen Valkyrja of Arom and her loyal sword, Ser Kilmister, rode out at the head of their army, ready to face whatever challenges lay ahead. Nevertheless, beneath his audacious exterior, a storm was brewing.

Time taunted Kilmister. Every year was a vindictive reminder of his doomed existence. It now seemed an endless punishment with no relief in sight. Each passing day amplified his yearning to feel the earth's kiss on his skin, the wind playfully rustling his hair, the thrill of a woman's touch. His admiration for Queen Valkyrja was morphing into resentment. These venomous thoughts bred an unexpected response within the valiant sword: a desire for blood and power.

The sword Kilmister had been witnessed by some of the soldiers the previous day, after the Queen had left him seated on the throne as she met with her Knights. The sentient sword sat atop the highest peak in the palace of stone, its blade shimmering with malevolent energy. A sinister grin seemed etched into its cold metal as it surveyed the world below with a twisted sense of satisfaction. The sword had long harbored a deep-seated hatred for all living beings, fueled by centuries of imprisonment and neglect.

After that, Kilmister, the sword, stayed unusually quiet by the side of the queen. Ordinarily, the metallic hum of his voice would be heard in council with the queen.

"You seem rather silent since our return to Arom. What worries you?" asked the Queen.

"No need to be concerned," he said in a metallic tone. "I have always spoken freely with your grace; may I do so now, Your Majesty?" answered the sword.

"Of course, there is no one I trust more."

"I want to see you dispatch our enemies with no mercy," he admitted.

"You wish to see me in battle?"

"You are an excellent Queen, your grace, but watching you as a warrior is an unmatched sight to see."

"Draknorr is dead. You killed him, but the Hrothgorn still breathe, and as we speak, they are reorganizing. Do not be bothered, my friend! We will strike before they set their eyes upon us," said the Queen.

Kilmister's experience of emotions had always been abstract, a mere echo of his human life. Now, anger and greed flooded him, a potent cocktail that tasted far too real and enticing. The notions of murder, deceit, and usurpation overpowered his thoughts, and the once loyal knight contemplated his Queen's delicate jugular under the sharp edge of his own blade.

An eerie undercurrent swam under Kilmister's sharp demeanor, sparking suspicions in the ominous court wizard, Odious Forge. Known for his prying nature and astute instincts, Forge sensed the shift in Kilmister's tone. He surmised that the trapped spirit was becoming restless, perhaps dangerous, and decided to intervene. His thoughts were interrupted abruptly.

Still out of breath, a messenger scrambled into the palace to the presence of the Queen.

"Your…majesty…I bring news from the North," the man wheezed. "Large companies of Hrothgorn are approaching the highroads."

"I knew it!" said Kilmister. "I could just feel it! We await your order, my Queen. We must ride out to meet them. They must know we…or you are there to stop them forever," said Kilmister.

"Call for Ser Dragonwülf!" ordered the Queen. "Together we will be unstoppable."

"If you and I were to go into battle, we would be indestructible, my queen," said Kilmister.

The Queen grasped the sword as a woman would grasp the hand of a man.

A courier approached the throne. "May I interrupt Your Grace? A large detachment of robed figures wishes to speak with Her Majesty."

"It is the Destiny of Tyr and Dragonwülf through the panorama of time. Let them enter at will. My Kingdom is their Kingdom.

The sword of Kilmister became more silent as the battle plans were drawn.

"I have never known you to be so speechless before, my sword exclaimed the Queen. "It is unnerving, to say the least."

"I am trying to control my anger and rage majesty," said Kilmister in his metallic voice.

"Anger and rage?" asked the Queen. "You have given me no indication of your dissatisfaction with me."

"I am not unhappy with your majesty. I just wish to remain quiet for a season. I am a man trapped in steel. I am no longer content with just being your sword. I want to be free. I was a slave to the Hrothgorn, and now I am a slave to the sword. Your majesty cannot blame me for being filled with rage."

"You will be needed for the battle to come. May I count on you?"

"You need not ask. I am always at your Service. I feel something unusual and disturbing within me."

"What is it you feel?"

"I feel a presence, an evil and dark shadow. I feel an encroaching wall of clouds and fire within me. I cannot escape its grasp. It calls to me for obedience."

"Why did you not make me aware of this before? I will try to help you make sense of it," said the queen.

"It makes no sense!" said Kilmister, raising his voice to the queen." I...am sorry, your Majesty. I do not know what is within me. I hear a voice that tells me that everyone and everything that has ever sought to destroy me will be tortured, clawed, and raked unto the pleading of death. They will whimper and beg like small children to their deaf mothers. I answer the same way each time and beg for mercy. You run through me, and I cannot escape your grasp. You are a vicious vampire of my soul!"

"Stay close to my side, Kilmister, and I will keep you safe. Do not worry. You kept me safe from our enemies in battle, and I will keep you safe now," promised the queen. I will tuck you under my wings and keep you warm and far from harm."

The court Wizard Odious Forge watched from a corner of the throne room and knew he must act soon. To verify his fears, he cast a spell, a forbidden enchantment to access the trapped thoughts of immortal objects. The practice was outlawed by King Tin'Old the first of his name to discourage the use of Necromancers. What he discovered was darker than his worst fears – betrayal, treachery, and murder. Forge, disturbed by this revelation, realized he had to intercept Kilmister at once.

Svæin the Elder, a royal advisor and confidant to Dragonwülf, rushed to the throne room to bring news to the queen. "Your majesty, the Hrothgorn is set yet again for battle. They lie just beyond the tree line!"

"What are their numbers? What weapons do they bear?"

"They have iron bulls and cannons. They use the same weapons as in the battles with Wolfclaw. There must be two or three thousand of the greasy ghouls!" said Svæin.

"What is our defense against this?" asked the Queen.

"I say let them come to us, and we will deliver pain and death to them. Let them come and get it from us. There is plenty to go around," said Svæin.

On the muddy battlefield leading to the gates of the city, the Hrothgorn set the cannons in a row. They were loaded with black powder and ready to fire.

The cannons were forged from Hrothgornian steel and carried on heavy wooden caissons held together with steel straps. The wooden wheels creaked and groaned under the weight of the cannons. Kor signaled to one of the officers.

"There are defectors running into the forest by the hundreds. Take a detachment, find them, and execute them. Bring me all of their heads. Forfeit yours if you miss any," ordered Kor.

"Yes, Ser, right away, Sir," said the officer as he turned and ran to do his General's bidding.

"The weakest part of the wall will be near the gates," said Kor.

"We shall set our cannons on the outer wall so we can have the advantage and destroy the enemy's walls also. We shall start there and work our way into the enemy's realm. We will crush them in the holes where they hide inside the caves."

The Battle of Arom

Ser Kilmister felt a deep anger and overwhelming angst coursing through his very being. Trapped within a magical sword, he could only communicate through a metallic ring voice that echoed ominously whenever he spoke. The once proud man was brought low by the dark circumstances in which he found himself.

The events leading to Ser Kilmister's current state were shrouded in mystery. He was a former slave of the Hrothgorn and was ensnared by a cursed sword that bound his soul to its blade. The Hrothgorn blacksmiths used the flesh of prisoners to test the white-hot blades of the newly forged swords. The odyssey of pain was so searing that the soul of Kilmister entered the steel of the sword, trapping his soul. He could feel the ominous approach of the Hrothgorn.

The Hrothgorn marched methodically. They were fearsome creatures with scales as black as night and eyes that glowed like fiery coals. They had amassed an army of dark creatures to conquer the peaceful realm.

In the towering halls of the Palace of Stone, Queen Valkyrja stood before her warriors, her voice resonating with both sorrow and determination. "Oh, my fierce warriors," she began, her silver armor gleaming under the golden light of the hall, "How I long to join you on the battlefield once more, to fight alongside you and feel the thrill of battle coursing through my veins. Rally the people!" Queen Valkyrja commanded her voice steady and strong. She stood tall and resolute, her golden armor gleaming in the sunlight as she surveyed the horizon where the enemy approached.

The people of Arom, armed with swords, spears, and bows, gathered around their queen, ready to defend their homeland against the impending threat. The air crackled with tension as the two armies faced each other across the battlefield, the evil Hrothgorn's forces outnumbering the defenders of Arom.

"You dare to challenge me, filthy palace dwellers? Look at yourselves and your riches!" General Kor's voice boomed across the battlefield, sending shivers down the spines of the bravest warriors. As Queen Valkyrja looked upon her warriors, her heart swelled with pride and longing. "Remember, my brave ones," she said. "I will always fight by your side, and my spirit soars with you on the battlefield. Together, we shall carve our names in the annals of history, a testament to the bond between queen and warrior. We may be outnumbered, but we fight with courage and honor!" Queen Valkyrja declared, For Arom! Her sword raised high.

With a mighty battle cry, the clash began. Swords clashed, arrows flew, and magic crackled in the air as the two forces collided in a fierce struggle for dominance. Hrothgorn's creatures, twisted and monstrous, fought with ruthless efficiency, but the people of Arom were driven by a fierce determination to protect their homeland.

As the battle raged on, Queen Valkyrja's skill with the sword of Kilmister was unmatched. She fought with grace and ferocity, cutting down enemy after enemy with expert precision. Her warriors fought bravely at her side, inspired by her leadership and unwavering courage.

"Is that the best you can do, Hrothgorn?" Queen Valkyrja taunted, her eyes flashing with defiance.

General Kor roared in fury, his eyes blazing with hatred. "I will crush you and your kingdom beneath my heel, Queen of the Snakes! You cannot defeat the might of Hrothgorn!"

Queen Valkyrja stood her ground, her determination unshakeable. With a final, desperate push, the forces of Arom surged forward, driving back the evil creatures of Hrothgorn until the battlefield was littered with fallen bodies and the air was thick with the scent of battle.

In the end, many Hrothgorn lay defeated, their dark army scattered and broken. Queen Valkyrja stood victorious, her sword dripping with the blood of her enemies, her eyes blazing with triumph.

"Retreat and regroup, cowardly maggots!" bellowed a defeated General Kor. "We will fight another day!"

With a solemn nod, the queen turned to enter the Palace hall once again, her cape billowing behind her like the wings of a Valkyrja in flight. As she walked away, her warriors stood, ready to face any challenge that came their way, knowing that their queen's spirit would always be with them, guiding them to victory.

Meanwhile, Kilmister, the sentient sword, grew darker.

"Darkness may consume my soul, but it is the world that shall drown in its depths, for when the night falls, and the shadows whisper my name, revenge shall be the melody that guides my hands to paint the world in hues of vengeance," he swore in a metallic voice that rang strangely like that of King Draknorr. "The world will pay for my sorrow with running blood.

The wizard Odious Forge knew he must act quickly.

Artifact Fourteen

Ópokkssmiðja ok djǫfulskló

(Odious Forge and the Demon Claw)

Dimension of Heimdall (32 BCE)

Under-forest Lands

Allir konungar verða at deyja.

All of the Kings must die.

Many years before the time of Queen Valkyrja in the eerie realm known as the Halls of Hel, where shadows danced ominously, and the air was thick with the scent of decay, Odious Forge found himself wandering aimlessly after being beheaded for the murder of the Prince Tin'Old not very long ago.

I cannot believe I must go through this horror again, he thought. In place of his head, he had packed a large white gauze bandage into the stump of his neck to staunch the blood. The ground beneath his feet was cold and damp, the walls covered in slimy moss that seemed to writhe and pulsate with a life of its own.

As he trudged through the dark corridors, Odious could hear the faint echoes of anguished wails and tortured screams that seemed to reverberate off the walls. The darkness seemed to swallow him whole, enveloping him in a suffocating embrace that sent shivers down his spine. Out of the cold, damp shadows stepped a terrifying figure known only as Ozymandias. A demon from the depths of the Halls of Hel sought an audience with the wizard Odious Forge. The demon's skin was as gray as the northern sky, and his eyes burned with an otherworldly fire. The air crackled with malevolent energy as the demon fixed his gaze upon Odious.

"I have been expecting you, wizard." Ozymandias's voice was a chilling whisper that seemed to seep into Odious' very soul. "You possess a power that intrigues me, a power that could tip the balance of existence."

Odious stood his ground, his own eyes flashing with a defiant spark. "What business do you have with me, demon of the underworld?

A twisted smile spread across Ozymandias's face, revealing rows of razor-sharp teeth. "I seek to forge an alliance, wizard. Together, we could wield a power that could shake the heavens and the hells alike."

The wizard's mind raced as he considered the demon's proposition.

Before Odious could respond, a wall of whispers filled the chamber, echoing with a sense of doom and destruction. The very walls seemed to groan in protest, as if unable to bear witness to the cosmic forces converging within their confines.

At that moment, Odious knew that his decision would shape the course of destiny itself. With a steely resolve, he met Ozymandias's gaze and spoke with unwavering conviction.

"I will not be swayed by your honeyed words, demon. My path is one of revenge and death, and no amount of power can tempt me from it."

Ozymandias's smile twisted into a snarl of fury, and the air crackled with dark energy. "So be it unto you, wizard. If you will not join me willingly, then you shall fall before me as so many others have."

"What could you grant me? I have no head, and my magic is spent?" asked the Wizard.

"I will grant you the ability to kill King Tin'Old of Arom and all of his successors down through the centuries."

"That is impossible, you forked tongue demon! The Prince is dead, and I was beheaded for his murder. The bloodline stops here, you fool!" said Odious.

"Your name-calling is very short-sighted. I have an answer and a bargain for you."

Despite his trepidation, Odious's curiosity was piqued. "Speak, demon. What is it that you seek from me?"

The demon's eyes seemed to smolder with a fiery intensity as it spoke, its words dripping with deceit. "I require a spell of untold power, one that will grant me dominion over the realms of the living and the dead. In exchange for your help, I offer you revenge upon your killer. I will agree to arrange a curse against all of the progeny of King Tin'Old that will send them to death before they become old. None will live past middle age."

"What of the Prince?" asked Odious.

"The Prince lives. The King has mistaken a lost farm boy for the Prince. Prince Tin'Old lives and will take the throne," explained Ozymandias.

Odious knew the dangers of dealing with creatures from the underworld, but the lure of such power was tempting. After a moment's hesitation, he spoke, his voice firm. "I will help you forge this spell, but know this: the realm of dark magic is no place for liars and thieves. Can I trust you not to betray me?"

"If you cannot trust a demon from the depths of the halls of Hel, who can you trust?" asked Ozymandias. "I will see to it that the Necromancer reunites you with your head, but I require a spell from your magic chest of wonders."

"I will do as you ask," said Odious. "First, a sacrifice must be made to show your worthiness to the incantation I will create."

"What sacrifice do you speak of, you liar? We had a deal."

"I must have a sacrifice! You will allow me to chop your clawed hand from the rest of your arm. Only that way can I trust your word," said Odious.

"Are you mad? Why would I consider such a thing?"

"You are a demon, Sir; you have seen worse in your realm alone," said Odious as he pulled a long dagger from beneath his cloak. With one movement from arm level, the dagger sliced the wrist of the demon, causing his clawed hand to drop to the floor like a fish on the deck of a boat.

A guttural howl pierced the stillness of the hall as the demon stumbled back, clutching its maimed limb.

"You dare to wound me, mortal?" Ozymandias roared, fury contorting its once-smug face.

Odious Forge stood his ground, a triumphant smile playing on his lips." I have my sacrifice," he declared, holding up the severed claw. "With this artifact, we will create a spell of great power."

The demon's eyes narrowed, a calculating gleam replacing the rage in its gaze. After a tense moment of silence, Ozymandias spoke in a voice laced with begrudging respect. "Very well, wizard. You have earned your prize."

Forge turned to the nearest column and held the claw of the demon high. "Oh, gods on high and the gods of the netherworld, hear me! Take this sacrifice of the demon claw and do with it what you will!" said Forge in an incantation. He raised the claw over his head, and with his dagger, he nailed it to the column.

As the final incantation was spoken, darkness unlike any other descended upon the Hall of Hel, twisting and warping reality itself.

At that moment, Odious realized the true extent of Ozymandias's treachery. With a malevolent laugh, the demon turned on the wizard, its form shifting and changing into a monstrous being of pure darkness.

"You fool, Odious Forge," Ozymandias taunted, his voice echoing with triumph. "You have served your purpose. Now, behold the power of the spell you helped create!"

As the darkness closed in around him, Odious knew that he had unleashed a force beyond his control. As the screams of the damned echoed through the halls of Hel, the wizard's fate was sealed in a pact of darkness and deceit.

Despite the chilling cold that seeped into his bones, Odious pressed on, determined to find a way out of this accursed place. He clutched the ghostly spirit of his severed head and the demon's claw tightly under his arm, the lifeless eyes staring blankly ahead, a constant reminder of the gruesome fate that had befallen him.

With each passing moment, the air grew thicker and the shadows darker, until Odious felt as though he was drowning in a sea of despair. The weight of his sins bore down on him heavily, dragging him further into the depths of his own guilt and remorse.

On the third day of his harrowing journey through the Halls of Hel, Odious heard a faint voice calling out to him from the darkness. He followed the sound, his heart pounding in his chest as he rounded a corner and came face to face with a hooded figure cloaked in shadows.

"Who goes there?" Odious demanded, his voice quivering with trepidation.

The figure raised its head, revealing a face shrouded in darkness, save for a pair of glowing red eyes that seemed to pierce through Odious' very soul. "I am the Necromancer summoned by your father, Eldon Void," the figure intoned in a voice like gravel grinding against stone. "I have come to offer you a second chance at life, Odious Forge."

With a mix of relief and disbelief, Odious followed the Necromancer through the bloody corridors of the Halls of Hel.

"Why in the name of Rothl'Orca would my father and the Destiny of Ty put me through this agony and torture again?" asked Forge.

"It is not for me to say or to question the Panorama of time. It is not within my realm. I can say one thing, this is the first time I have seen you," said the Necromancer. "You have slept with Demons, and now you will pay what is due. You hold the Demon claw, and now you are in his debt."

Rivers of old blood crept along the black stone like living veins, pooling beneath pillars carved from the bones of forgotten gods. The air was thick with iron and ash, and the screams of the eternally damned whispered through the vaulted corridors like a breath drawn by the underworld itself.

In the center of the Bloody Hall lay a body. As Forge looked down through his ghost head, he beheld the body of himself.

Odious Forge.

Once the greatest sorcerer to kneel before a throne, now sprawled across the obsidian floor, his robes were shredded, his chest split by ancient runes burned backward into his flesh. His right hand still twitched, fingers clawing at nothing.

Several paces away, his head rested upright upon a *spike of black iron.*

Its eyes were open, and they burned like celestial flame.

"Is this truly the end, then?" the head rasped, lips cracking into a smile. "Beheaded by a king with a mistaken death warrant and a borrowed sword from a Knight?"

A shadow shifted.

"Do not worry, Forge. I have this in my control," said the headless Forge.

"Do not speak," the Necromancer warned.

But Odious Forge was already chanting.

The blood lifted in strands, threading through the air like crimson wire. The wizard's severed body jerked, spine arching unnaturally as unseen forces dragged it upright.

Forge took a step back.

"By Tyr's broken oath…"

"Too late," Odious Forge hissed. "The King cut my neck, not my will."

The iron spike groaned as the head tore itself free, floating—*floating*—toward the body. Vertebrae snapped into alignment. Tendons knitted like black silk. Flesh flowed and sealed, leaving a jagged scar that glowed with hellfire runes.

Odious Forge inhaled deeply and ecstatically.

He rolled his shoulders, testing the reconnection, then turned his burning gaze upon the king.

"Did you truly believe," he said softly, "that kings are allowed to kill men like me?" Odious Forge raised both hands. The halls went silent.

Even the damned stopped screaming.

"Hear me, Hel," the wizard intoned. "Hear me, Hades and executioners, hear me, forgotten dead who died beneath crowns."

He turned slowly, addressing not only Tin'Old through the corridors of time but every throne that had ever existed.

Then he spoke. "Hear the words of the Necromancer through the panorama and throughout all eternity. Hear him!"

Odious Forge's voice was now the voice of the Necromancer, layered and ancient, as the runes on his flesh ignited.

"Rækh-thorûn val'kyras, shaal mor'drevan."

(Kings of the world, hear your damnation.)

"Vael sarnûm draegoth, vael krûn-deva shathra,"

(By the blood of the slain, by the broken bones of gods,)

"Kha'thronas velrûn ashka'rai."

(I turn your crowns to ash.)

"Naer rex vel'surath."

(No king shall be safe.)

"Vael-dae morrak, glaedh et faminek shaal-trûn."

(From this day forth, blade and famine shall follow you.)

"Imperath mor'kael. Thraenûm ruun'kar."

(Empires shall fall. Thrones shall crumble.)

"Ego…" *(he corrects himself, voice warping)*

"Zhal am Kûrath."

(I am the curse.)

"Zhal am Finûr-Ræx."

(I am the end of kings.)

The spell detonated outward.

Somewhere in the living world, crowns cracked. Thrones shuddered. Kings woke screaming, clutching their throats.

The darkness parted before them like a curtain being drawn aside. As they emerged into the blinding light, Odious felt a sense of anger and revenge wash over him, knowing that he had been given a chance to redeem himself and make Kings and Queens pay for their misdeeds.

The Kings and Queens must die.

Artifact Fifteen

Morguneldr himins

ᛗᛟᚱᚷᚢᚾᛏᛗᛚᛞᚱ ᚺᛗᛁᛗᛖᛁᛏᛋ

(Morning Fire of the Sky)

Dimension of Óðinn (126 AD)

"He who fights too long against dragons becomes a dragon himself; and if you gaze too long into the abyss, the abyss will gaze into you."

-Friedrich Nietzsche

The Council of the Destiny of Tyr, an omnipotent assembly governing the fates of warriors, decided to set a meeting to discuss a gift for the legendary Dragonwülf.

"Dragonwülf has been tirelessly fighting the legions of darkness, defending the weak, and upholding our name," declared Óðinn, the highest of all gods. "We will reward him with something special from us, a gift from on high."

"He indeed does," agreed Freya, the goddess of love and war. "But what can we give him that suits his strength and spirit?"

"He must have a mount befitting a warrior of his caliber?" suggested Tyr.

Everyone agreed with his suggestion, but the challenge was, what creature could carry a legend such as Dragonwülf? After hours of intense debate and scrutiny, an agreement was finally reached. They decided to give Dragonwülf a dragon as an enchanted gift.

"True," said Óðinn, "Nothing could be a more fitting companion for Dragonwülf. A dragon is the mightiest creature of the skies!"

The dragon they chose was a majestic beast known for its radiant silver scales and a thundering roar. The dragon also respected Dragonwülf's valor and heart and willingly agreed to accompany him into the tremendous battles.

On a chilling winter night, the council summoned Dragonwülf. He emerged from a column of swirling golden light, his eyes wide in awe as he looked around the grandeur of the Council. Óðinn, the highest of the gods, addressed him with words filled with pride and respect.

"Dragonwülf, your bravery and valor have won our hearts. As a token of our appreciation, we offer you the mightiest dragon to be your loyal companion. Ride her into the battles and let your enemies cower in fear."

In a flash of light and a crunch of thunder, a massive gray-scaled dragon appeared in the middle of the throne room of the Palace of Stone. She breathed with a choking breath of fire and belched phosphorus. Her eyes glowed red as she shifted her weight to her haunches and sat upright. The beast's mouth was a shiny, fluid-covered array of jagged teeth and drooling saliva. From the massive head to the tail, her dorsal fin was a sharp row of knife-like fins capable of causing death and injury. Dragonwülf was startled, grasped his sword, and pulled it from its sheath, pointing it at the great beast. "Stand where you are, you demon of death, or I will lay your gut open like a fish!"

Queen Valkyrja pulled Kilmister and pointed him directly at the heart of the dragon. "Come for us, and you will have two swords in your belly!" said the Queen.

"Wait!" ordered Avat'or. "This is the answer to your battle now and the wars to come, Dragonwülf. You are now a dragon rider. This beast was meant to be a gift, not an enemy! This ancient art has been restored unto you by the Destiny of Tyr. Her name is 'Morning-fire of the Sky.' She is your dragon. Use her wisely, and she will serve you well. Abuse her, and she will kill you if we do not get to you first."

"I cannot ride a dragon! Are you daft?" said a shocked Dragonwülf.

"Yes, you may. She will only allow *you* to ride her. No one else will be so gifted."

Dragonwülf walked slowly around the great beast and apprehensively approached her from the front. The dragon's breath was hot and overpowering, but the old warrior trusted the Destiny of Tyr.

"Walk behind her, and she will put you on her back with her tail," instructed Avat'or.

"What then? What should I do then?" he asked with a shaky voice.

"Hold on, I suppose," said Avat'or with a chuckle in his voice.

Just as Destiny had said, the giant creature gently placed Dragonwülf on her back just below her head and rose into the sky through the open courtyard. The members of the queen's court could hear the warrior screaming into the sky.

From the tree line outside the kingdom gates, General Kor witnessed the first ride of Dragonwülf. "What in the name of Róthul-Orkr is that?" asked Kor.

"I believe it is a dragon," replied an officer.

"I know that! You fool! The next time you see it, shoot it out of the sky. If you miss it, go and throw yourself from the tower!"

Kor shook his head in disbelief as he gazed at the majestic beast that had suddenly appeared before him. After a moment of awe, he realized that this was no ordinary dragon. Now it had become the mount of the ancient warrior Wolfclaw Thur'Gold, now known as Dragonwülf, the enemy of Hrothgorn!

The General had heard the stories of Dragonwülf, and now his enemy had been gifted a dragon to ride into battle against the Hrothgorn forces. It was as if ancient stories of bravery and battle told by elders about a fearless warrior of the distant past were coming to fruition right before his eyes.

Kor felt a surge of admiration for the mighty creature before him. He knew Dragonwülf was a true warrior, worthy of champion status. He realized that he was witnessing a moment in history, one that would be remembered for centuries to come. He turned to the officer beside him and said, "Gather the men; we are about to pursue Dragonwülf into battle and deliver him to his death!"

The men of Kor's army roared with delight.

The Dragon Rider of Arom

Dragonwülf was obviously known for his bravery and unmatched skills in battle, but now he found himself facing a new challenge. It was a challenge not of swordsmanship or combat but of a different kind. It was the challenge of mastering the art of riding a dragon.

Dragonwülf swallowed hard as he faced the fearsome dragon directly at eye level. He came face to face with her jagged, toothy array. This majestic creature had scales as dark as night and eyes that glowed like embers. With wings that spanned wide and a power that shook the very earth, Morning Fire was a remarkable sight.

As Dragonwülf climbed onto the dragon's back again, he felt a rush of excitement and apprehension. *I must have more control this time*, he thought. He had heard tales of the bond between dragon and rider, of the unspoken connection that allowed them to soar through the skies as one. He knew that mastering this bond would require more than just strength and courage. It would require trust, respect, and understanding.

"Easy now, Morning Fire," Dragonwülf said softly, his voice calm and steady. "We are in this together, you and me. Let us show the world what we are capable of doing.

"I will do as you wish," said the Dragon.

"Wait! You can speak. How is it possible that you have words and ideas?" asked an incredulous Dragonwülf. "Why did they not tell me this? It would have been good to know!"

The beast answered, "I was enchanted by The Destiny. I am one of a kind. There are no others like me."

With a powerful beating of her wings, the creature launched into the sky. At first, the ride was exhilarating but chaotic. The dragon's movements were wild and unpredictable, and Dragonwülf struggled to find his balance.

"Steady now, girl," Dragonwülf called out, his words firm but gentle. "We must move as one, guided by trust and respect."

As they soared higher and higher, Dragonwülf began to feel the rhythm of Morning Fire's movements. He learned to anticipate her turns and adjust his position accordingly. With each passing moment, their bond grew stronger until it felt as though they were truly one being.

"Look, Morning Fire," Dragonwülf exclaimed, pointing to a distant mountain peak. "Let us race to the summit and claim victory together!"

With a roar of agreement, "Hold on tight, old one!" Morning Fire surged forward, her wings beating against the wind with power and grace. Together, they pushed themselves to the limit, flying faster and higher than ever before.

As they reached the mountain peak, Dragonwülf let out a triumphant shout, his heart pounding with exhilaration. He had mastered the art of riding a dragon, not through force or domination, but through mutual respect and understanding.

"Thank you, Morning Fire," Dragonwülf said, his voice filled with gratitude. "Together, we are unstoppable."

"We will see. You have much to learn," answered Morning Fire. "I will teach you, and then we will be invincible together."

Artifact Sixteen

The Battle of Val'goz

Dimension of Óðinn 126 CE
Underforest Lands

"There are more powerful things in Hell than on Earth,"
-Val'goz

Morning Fire of the Sky became a creature of legends, with shimmering scales that glowed like molten gold in the sunlight. Her wings were as vast as the clouds themselves, and her breath could melt even the hardest ice. Dragonwülf and Morning Fire became inseparable, bound by a bond that went beyond words.

As her training with Dragonwülf continued, a cry for help reached their ears. A village nestled at the foot of the mountains was under attack by a band of marauding raiders, their homes ablaze and their people in peril. Without hesitation, Dragonwülf and Morning plunged toward the village, ready to unleash their fury upon the enemies of the innocent.

As they swooped down from the heavens, Dragonwülf's voice rang out like thunder, commanding the raiders to retreat or face the wrath of the dragon. The raiders, taken aback by the sight of the fearsome dragon, hesitated for a moment before regaining their courage and launching their attack.

With a mighty roar, Morning Fire belched forth a stream of searing flames that engulfed the raiders in an inferno of destruction. Dragonwülf, his blade flashing in the sunlight, leaped from the dragon's back and cut a path through the enemy ranks with the skill of a true warrior.

"Feel the fury of the dragon's breath, you cowardly beasts!" Dragonwülf's voice echoed across the battlefield, striking fear into the hearts of his enemies. The raiders, their ranks decimated and their will broken, fled in terror before the might of Dragonwülf.

His eyes blazed with determination as he spoke, his voice deep and commanding. "You have brought destruction to these lands for the last time. Today, you will face the wrath of Dragonwülf, the blood of dragons!"

With a roar that shook the very earth, Morning Fire unleashed a torrent of flames upon the raiders, engulfing them in a blazing inferno. The raiders cried out in terror as they were consumed by the dragon's fiery breath, their weapons melting in the intense heat.

The townspeople looked into the sky with a combination of awe and fear as they watched Morning Fire rise into the sky.

Later that day, in the depths of a vast cavern with shimmering crystals adorning the walls, Dragonwülf stood face to face with his loyal companion. The majestic dragon towered over Dragonwülf, its iridescent scales reflecting the flickering light of the torches that lined the cave.

"Today, my friend, we shall embark on a training session unlike any other. Today you will learn to make war," Dragonwülf announced, his voice echoing through the cavern. His dragon let out a rumbling growl of approval, her fiery breath dancing across the rocky ground.

"You must also let me train you in *my ways,*" she said.

The warrior and the dragon began their training, their movements fluid and precise as they danced around each other in perfect harmony. Dragonwülf wielded his sword with grace and skill, each strike landing with deadly accuracy. Meanwhile, Morning Fire of the Sky unleashed torrents of flames that devoured the air with searing heat.

As they sparred, Dragonwülf and Morning Fire communicated not with words, but with a silent understanding that transcended language. The warrior anticipated the dragon's movements, while the dragon responded to Dragonwülf's commands with unwavering loyalty.

Their training continued for hours; the intensity of their practice matched only by the fierce bond that united them. Sweat glistened on Dragonwülf's brow as he pushed himself to his limits, his determination unwavering.

Morning Fire of the Sky roared with excitement, her eyes gleaming with pride at its warrior companion's prowess.

At last, as the sun began to set outside the crystal cavern, Dragonwülf and Morning Fire of the Sky came to a halt, their chests heaving with exertion. "Well fought, my friend," Dragonwülf said, his voice filled with admiration. "Together, we are unstoppable."

Dragonwülf gazed ahead with a furrowed brow, his steely eyes filled with determination." The reason that The Destiny of Tyr has placed you and me together is to search for and stop the renegade, Defiler, before he unleashes chaos upon our world," he said, his voice firm and resolute.

"I stand by your side. Together, we will bring an end to him," she replied, her fiery voice resonating with power.

With a powerful beat of her wings, Morning Fire took to the sky, her mighty form soaring gracefully through the air as Dragonwülf mounted her back, his sword glinting in the fading light. As they flew over the treetops, the wind whistling in their ears, Dragonwülf spoke to his dragon companion.

"I have heard whispers of one of the Defiler's demons from Hell hiding in the ancient ruins to the north, where he trains more followers to join the Defiler," Dragonwülf said, his voice tinged with urgency.

"A training camp for Demons?" asked Morning Fire.

"Yes, let us make haste and stop him before the Defiler's numbers grow," said Dragonwülf.

Morning Fire inclined her head, her eyes focused ahead. "I sense his malevolent presence, Dragonwülf. He is a dangerous," she replied, her voice filled with a touch of fear for Dragonwulf's well-being.

As they neared the ruins, a dark shadow loomed over them, and a sinister laughter filled the air. Val'goz, the demon, emerged from the shadows, his eyes glowing with a malevolent light.

"Who demands entrance to my domain?" asked the demon.

"It is I, Dragonwülf and Morning Fire, sent by The Destiny of Tyr."

"Who is the Destiny that should have dominion over me?" hissed the demon.

"We mean to send you back to Hell where you belong," said Dragonwülf, reaching for the bone handle of his sword.

Dragonwülf gripped his sword tightly, his eyes narrowed in determination. "Your reign of terror ends here, foul creature. We will not allow you to bring harm to our world," he declared, his voice echoing through the ruins.

Val'goz bellowed an order to his many students of evil surrounding him. "*Daemones, nunc venite* (Come at once, demons).

The demons dropped from the ceiling of the hellish cavern and clashed with Morning Fire in a fierce battle that shook the very foundations of the forest. Fire and shadow intertwined, casting light and darkness across the land. The dragon's roars reverberated through the trees, each breath a torrent of flames that scorched the earth.

"Bring me death, creatures of darkness!" Morning Fire's voice boomed, shaking the demons to their core. "Know that you face not just a dragon, but all of the gods in Asgard!"

Val'goz sneered, its eyes gleaming with wicked delight.

"We fear no dragon, no matter how powerful. The shadows will consume all in the end. There are more powerful things in Hell than on Earth," said Val'goz.

With a deafening battle cry, Dragonwülf leaped from his dragon and charged toward the demons, his sword gleaming in the dim light. The clash of steel against claw filled the air as the ancient warrior fought with unparalleled skill and ferocity. His movements were a deadly dance, each strike calculated and precise.

"Die!" a demon screeched, launching itself at Dragonwülf with reckless, uncontrolled violence.

Dragonwülf was faster, his blade slicing through the demon's flesh with a swift and lethal arc. The creature howled in agony before dissolving into a pile of blackened ash.

As the battle raged on, Dragonwülf's strength seemed inexhaustible. His eyes blazed with fierce determination as he vanquished demon after demon, each victory fueling his resolve.

"You cannot defeat us. We have been here since the beginning of time, and we will be here forever!" a demon snarled, its bloodstained claws reaching for the warrior's throat.

With a mighty roar, Dragonwülf delivered a final blow, cleaving the demon in two with a single stroke. The remaining demons hesitated, their resolve wavering in the face of such overwhelming power.

"You have underestimated me, foul creatures. Now face my wrath!" he thundered, his voice echoing through the cavern like a thunderclap.

In a flurry of movement, Dragonwülf launched a devastating onslaught, driving the demons back with relentless force. The forest shook with the intensity of the battle as the ancient warrior fought with terrible intensity.

When the last demon fell, defeated and broken, Dragonwülf stood victorious amidst the carnage, his chest heaving with exertion.

Dragonwülf lowered his bloodied sword, a sense of weary satisfaction settling upon him. As a second wave of the creatures descended upon them, Morning Fire launched herself at the demon lord, claws slashing through the air like knives. The demons swarmed around the dragon, their dark forms twisting and writhing in a grotesque dance of death.

The battle raged on with Dragonwülf back high atop Morning Fire, the cavern becoming a battleground of fire and shadow. The earth trembled, and the skies darkened with the intensity of their clash. Morning Fire fought with all her might, her scales gleaming like molten gold as she unleashed her full power upon the demons.

Then Val'goz let out a menacing laugh, his form shifting and changing as dark energy crackled around him. "You are too late, fools. My power grows stronger with each second of time," he taunted, his voice sending shivers down their spines.

With a roar of defiance, Morning Fire unleashed a torrent of flames upon Val'goz, the scorching heat engulfing him in a fiery inferno. Dragonwülf charged forward, his sword flashing in the darkness, as he struck the demon's throat with his dagger. As the ruins of the demon crumbled around them, Dragonwülf stood victorious, the threat of Val'goz the demon finally destroyed.

"The Defiler awaits us, Morning Fire," said Dragonwülf.

"We will not disappoint him," said the dragon.

"We must meet with the Deepwater Watchman as fast as your wings will carry us. Only then can we jump through the panorama of time to find the Defiler."

Artifact Seventeen

The Redemption of Odious Forge

Dimension of Óðinn 126 CE

Underforest Lands

"Would you please stand still, Wizard? How am I supposed to kill you if you keep moving?" – King Draknorr

Dragonwülf returned to the Deepwater Watchman with his majestic dragon companion. As the sun rose over the horizon, painting the sky in hues of pink and orange, Dragonwülf began his daily training routine with Morning Fire.

Together, they soared through the clouds, their bond unbreakable as they practiced intricate aerial maneuvers and perfected their synchronization in battle. Dragonwülf's movements were fluid and precise, a true display of his connection with Morning Fire. The dragon's fiery breath illuminated the sky as they executed each move flawlessly, a remarkable sight for any onlooker.

As they trained tirelessly, a dark shadow loomed over the kingdom in the form of the sword Kilmister, a powerful sword known for its heroic deeds. Rumors whispered of his recent fury, driving him to madness. The curse of Kilmister spread like wildfire, leaving a trail of destruction in its wake.

The Wizard Odious Forge stood before the Queen in the presence of Kilmister to try to reason with the Queen.

"Your majesty, I have come to you about a rather urgent issue concerning Ser Kilmister," he said, assuming the Queen would be receptive.

Unknown to all, including the Queen, Forge held a sinister secret - the involvement of the royal family. The curse of Odious Forge ran deep, entwined with the history of her ancestors. The deal he had made with the demon Ozymandias centuries before had been broken by his own hand when the Queen came to power. There was but one who knew the secret, Kilmister, the living sword.

In shock and disbelief, the Queen discovered through the whisperings of Kilmister the murderous deeds committed by Forge. He killed all of the royal family, starting with her beloved grandfather, King Geir'wolf Tin'Old I, the lost Prince Geir'wolf, before he was King Tin'Old II, the Cowardly King, and the Queen's brother, Tin'Old III. The betrayal cut deep, a wound that tore at the very fabric of her being. The Queen vowed to seek justice for her family.

"Queen Valkyrja of Arom stood in her chambers, her eyes blazing with fury as she confronted her court wizard, Odious Forge." Clear the chamber! I want no others here. The wizard and I have business alone." She sat on her throne and leaned forward on the arm. She thought quietly for a moment. "I trusted you as a friend, but you are a fiend!" she said, staring into the wizard's eyes. You murdered my entire lineage of Kings! Explain yourself, and then I will unleash my full wrath of a sentence upon you!"

Odious Forge knelt before the queen, his head bowed in shame. "Majesty, I was consumed by revenge. I succumbed to the temptations of wrath. I was executed for the death of Prince Tin'Old when he could not be located. The body of a boy was found, and the King thought it to be the Prince. He took my head shortly before the Prince was found alive."

"I was to be your next victim, you treacherous cutthroat?" the Queen asked with anger. "All of the times I trusted you, and I was to be murdered also?"

"It *was* meant to be, but I knew because of my love for you and our time together with the Fellowship of Wolfclaw that the curse would and should be broken. After the battle with the Hrothgorn at the cliffs of Athgor, I threw my body to the rocks below. I am full of sorrow for my deeds.

The queen's hand grasped the hilt of her sword, her voice cold as steel. "Your false sorrow will not bring back the Kings of my bloodline. You have tarnished the honor of our kingdom and disgraced us all. For your treachery, you shall face justice." Pausing for a brief time, the Queen asked, "The King took your head, and you dashed yourself upon the rocks below the cliffs. How is it that you stand before me alive?"

"My father performed dark magic and reunited me with my head. The Destiny of Tyr resurrected me a second time to serve them. I cannot die. I wish to, but I cannot!"

"It is a shame to waste good magic, for I am going to behead you again. Guards seize this ghoul and await my arrival in the courtyard for sentencing!"

The wizard raised his head, a glint of defiance in his eyes. "Queen Valkyrja, I accept whatever punishment you deem fit for my crimes. The darkness that consumed me still lurks within our kingdom. There is someone who seeks power and will stop at nothing to seize the throne."

"Speak, you treacherous fool, before I loosen your tongue for you!" ordered the Queen.

"Your Majesty," Forge began, his voice filled with urgency, "I have made a discovery of grave importance that threatens the very foundation of our kingdom."

Queen Valkyrja leaned forward, her emerald eyes fixed on the wizard. "Speak, fool, what have you uncovered? I believe you may be trying to delay your death! "

Odious cleared his throat, the weight of his words hanging heavy in the air. "It is the living sword, Kilmister, my Queen. It harbors a sinister plot to unleash chaos upon our land and murder you!"

Queen Valkyrja's brow furrowed in disbelief. Kilmister? Do not be ridiculous. He is with me always and my most trusted confidant."

The wizard paced the chamber, his cloak billowing behind him like a shadow. "I have delved deep into my ancient spell and incantations and discovered that Kilmister seeks to destroy you, my Queen, and claim the throne for himself. He is possessed by a very familiar evil."

The Queen's eyes widened with realization, a cold shiver running down her spine. At the same time, she could feel the metal of the sword becoming exceedingly hot.

"But how could a mere sword possess such treacherous intentions?" she asked while barely being able to touch her sword.

Odious paused, meeting her gaze with a steely resolve. "The magic that binds Kilmister is dark and ancient, fueled by a desire for power that knows no bounds. It sees you as the only obstacle to its ambitions. I believe it is the spirit of King Draknorr."

A booming, dark voice filled the chamber. The tapestries on the walls of the palace began to shake violently. Kilmister, the sword jumped from the hands of the Queen. He emitted a metallic shriek and hurled his sword body at Odious Forge, narrowly missing him and tearing through his robe.

"Let them tremble at the sound of my name, let them cower in fear at the sight of my gaze. I am the embodiment of their nightmares and the manifestation of their sins. When the flames of retribution consume this world, they will know that it was I who brought about their downfall," bellowed Kilmister. "I am your worst nightmare. I am *Draknorr* returned. I am still the ruler of the Hrothgorn and your scourge!" The sword once again aimed for Forge and struck a glancing blow against his shoulder, opening up a wound.

"Would you please stand still, Wizard? How am I supposed to *kill you* if you keep moving?" asked Draknorr. "You are a pathological coward. You squandered the opportunity to kill the Queen and everyone around her, but instead chose to dive headlong into a canyon. You are a pathetic fool! You could have been a memorable assassin or a King killer, but you wasted it."

"Where is Kilmister, Draknorr? How many times do we have to kill you? We destroyed your Palace and killed your army! Why will you not die?" asked the Queen.

"You ask too many questions! I do not feel obliged to answer them. Kilmister is trapped in here with me. I have him bound, and I am most definitely going to kill him. He is weak and too loyal to you. I refuse to die until I have my revenge on the one they call Wolfclaw Thur'Gold. He is known as Dragonwülf."

"I do not know him. You waste your time looking here among us for him," said the Queen.

"I *will rake* through this entire Kingdom with the edge of my sword. I will claw through person by person until he is found," threatened Draknorr. "I will practice my flaying technique on those who dare to hide Dragonwülf from me."

"Your Majesty, your path is fraught with peril, but heed my counsel, and you shall emerge victorious," said Forge. "King Draknorr's heart is as black as the abyss, filled with malice and deceit. Beware, for his magic is as deadly as his tongue."

Determined to face his nemesis, Draknorr pressed onward, his blade gleaming with righteous fury. At last, he reached Odious Forge, surrounded by a swirling maelstrom of dark energy.

With a thunderous clash, the battle between the living sword and the dark wizard erupted in a symphony of magic and steel. Lightning cracked across the sky as the blade danced with unmatched precision, deflecting the wizard's dark spells with unwavering resolve.

The sword gleamed with an otherworldly light, its edges pulsating with malevolence, and it hungered for destruction.

Odious held his staff aloft, its crystal tip shimmering with a pure, white light that cut through the shadows like a beacon of hope. He stood tall and resolute, his eyes fixed upon the malevolent sword that floated before him, a storm of magic crackling between them.

"Your powers are weak, wizard?" boomed King Draknorr, his voice a thunderous growl that shook the very foundations of the forest. "I am the rightful ruler of this land, and no one can stand against me!"

Odious smiled with a note of defiance in his eyes. "Your threats fall on deaf ears, Draknorr."

With a wordless roar, King Draknorr swung his enchanted sword in a wide arc, sending a wave of dark energy hurtling toward Odious. The wizard raised his staff in response, a shield of pure magic forming around him just in time to absorb the impact. The force of the blow sent Odious stumbling backward, his boots digging into the soft earth beneath him.

"Is that the best you can do, wizard?" sneered King Draknorr, his eyes gleaming with malice. "I expected more from one who fancies himself an ancient purveyor of dark magic."

Odious steadied himself, his expression steely. He whispered an incantation under his breath, and the ground beneath Draknorr's feet began to tremble. Roots and vines sprang forth from the earth, entangling the evil king in a web of nature's wrath.

Enraged, Draknorr wrenched himself free with a mighty roar, his sword blazing with dark fire. He charged towards Odious, his every step shaking the earth with the force of his malice. Odious stood his ground, his staff raised high, and a defiant gleam in his eyes.

The two opponents clashed in a whirlwind of magic and steel, their blows ringing out like thunder through the forest. Sparks flew as the enchanted sword met the wizard's staff in a symphony of light and darkness. Each strike sent shockwaves rippling through the air, the very fabric of reality warping and twisting in their wake.

As the battle raged on, Odious felt the raw power of the sword pressing down upon him, its malevolent aura threatening to overwhelm his defenses. He refused to yield, drawing upon the depths of his magic in a desperate bid to turn the tide.

With a final, mighty incantation, Odious channeled all his remaining strength into a blinding burst of light that engulfed King Draknorr and his malevolent sword.

As the conflict raged on, the very fabric of reality trembled under the weight of their struggle. The Queen, who had unwittingly set the wheels of fate in motion, watched in awe as Odious Forge fought with a valor unmatched by any hero of legend.

In a final, decisive strike, Draknorr's sword Kilmister plunged his blade deep into Odious Forge's heart, shattering the wizard's soul and revealing the presence of King Draknorr in the sword. With a defiant roar, the wizard crumbled to dust, his dark legacy forever disappearing from the realm.

"Now, *Your Majesty,* let us address the matter at hand. Deliver Dragonwülf to me. Please do not dare to feign ignorance about where he resides. I will have him," said Draknorr.

"I will never reveal to you his whereabouts even if I knew."

"You *will,* foolish Queen. *I promise* you will."

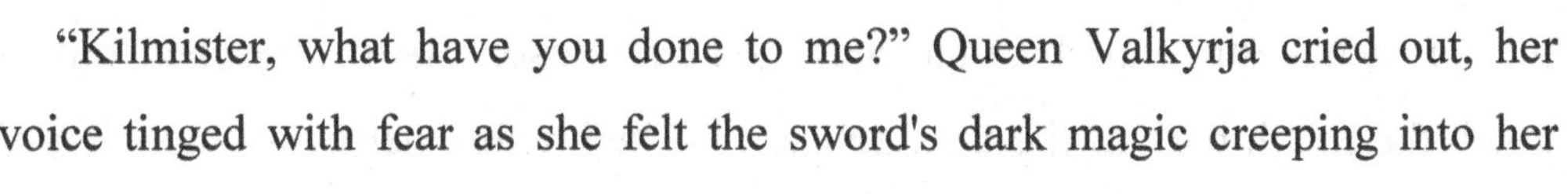

"Kilmister, what have you done to me?" Queen Valkyrja cried out, her voice tinged with fear as she felt the sword's dark magic creeping into her mind.

"Do not resist, my queen," the sword's voice echoed in her mind, its tone dripping with malice. "You belong to me now, and together, we shall conquer all who dare oppose us."

Determined to break free from Kilmister's hold, Queen Valkyrja knew she had to find a way to rid herself of the cursed sword's influence. With a heavy heart and a mind filled with desperation, she set out on a perilous journey through the Enchanted Forest, guided by a flicker of hope and the whispers of ancient spirits.

As she ventured deeper into the heart of the forest, Queen Valkyrja stumbled upon a hidden clearing bathed in shimmering moonlight. There, standing tall and proud against the backdrop of towering trees, was the ancient tree spirits she had encountered as a young girl.

"We have been expecting you, our Queen Valorii Thuireld," said one of the spirits.

"You remember me?" she asked. "I have not been known by that name for many seasons."

"We have never left you in our spirits, and we are always ready to be of Service to you, our Queen.

Approaching the sacred trees, Queen Valkyrja heard a soft, melodic hum in the air, a haunting lullaby that beckoned her closer. As she reached out to touch the rough bark of the tree, a vision flashed before her eyes – a vision of the cursed sword, Kilmister, buried deep within the forest floor, its dark magic sealed away for eternity.

Determined to break free from the sword's grasp, Queen Valkyrja knew what she had to do. With trembling hands and a heart filled with resolve, she drew Kilmister from its sheath and raised it high above her head.

"What vision you have seen, you must do," said the tree spirit

"No!" the sword screamed in defiance, its voice filled with rage and desperation. "You cannot defy me, mortal! I am eternal!"

Ignoring the sword's protests, Queen Valkyrja brought Kilmister crashing down upon the forest floor, the ground trembling beneath her feet as the earth swallowed the cursed blade whole. A blinding light erupted from the spot where Kilmister had been buried, illuminating the clearing in a dazzling display of magic.

As the light faded and silence descended upon the forest once more, Queen Valkyrja felt a weight lift from her shoulders, a sense of peace and freedom washing over her. The cursed sword, Kilmister, possessed by the soul of a dead King Draknorr, was silenced through the power of the tree spirits.

With a grateful heart and a renewed sense of purpose, Queen Valkyrja returned to her kingdom, ready to face whatever challenges lay ahead. The Enchanted Forest whispered its thanks in the wind, its ancient spirits watching over her with quiet reverence.

Artifact Eighteen

"Hǫnd dróttningar"
The Hand of the Queen

Dimension of Óðinn (126 CE)

"Your Majesty, you have more bravery and spirit than even the fiercest soldier!"

Ser Svæin, the warrior and trusted advisor to both Queen Valkyrja and Dragonwülf, walked quietly up to his Queen as she was in contemplative thought.

"Your Majesty…it is time to go. I assume I will be joining you in some more heroic exploits," he said tongue-in-cheek.

"No, Svæin, you will not be accompanying me this time," answered the Queen.

"I protest, Majesty! I am old, but I have more battle in me than four younger men," he protested. "Why would you leave me here?"

"The things you say are true. If I am not to return from my search for General Kor, I desire one of the people whom I will trust and bravely serve as the King of Arom.

"What do you mean, Your Grace?" asked Svæin.

"I mean to leave you in charge of the Kingdom as the hand of the Queen and King in waiting if I lose my life in battle with the Hrothgorn. I can think of no one better suited to help the common man than you," said the Queen.

"I do not know what to say, my Queen… Thank you for your trust in me."

"Just say yes, and I will return to our Kingdom soon. Choose your own Knights from among those you trust and swear their allegiance to the Palace," said the Queen.

A messenger hurriedly ran into the courtyard. "There is a pigeon dent from our forward scouts beyond the Sea of Arom. The Hrothgorn in platoons of thousands are on the move to the north by way of the sea," said the messenger.

"We must stop them before they mount the great sea," said the Queen.

"I swell with pride when I think about what you have become. When our Dragonwülf and I spotted you as a young girl following our war party, I was against you joining us at sixteen years old because I thought you were a weak little girl. I am so sorry, Your Majesty. You have more bravery and spirit than even the fiercest soldier!"

"We defeated the Hrothgorn then, and we can do it together again, brave Svæin," said the Queen.

"Queen Valkyrja, the time has come for you to depart for battle," Ser Svæin stated, his voice firm and resolute as he stood before the Queen in the grand courtyard of the castle.

"I trust in your abilities to rule in my absence, Ser Svæin," the Queen replied, her eyes filled with determination. "Protect the Kingdom with all your might."

"I shall not fail you, my Queen," Ser Svæin vowed, his hand placed over his heart in a gesture of loyalty. "The Kingdom shall be safe under my watch."

Queen Valkyrja nodded, a sense of pride swelling in her chest as she looked upon her trusted warrior. "I entrust you with the safety of our people, Ser Svæin. Do not hesitate to make difficult decisions in my absence."

"I will do my utmost, my Queen," Ser Svæin replied, his gaze unwavering as he bowed before her. "May the gods grant you victory in battle to do more than your utmost!"

With a final nod, Queen Valkyrja turned towards her magnificent ship, ready to embark on her quest to face the menacing Hrothgorn. As she began to ascend the gangplank, she cast one last glance back at Ser Svæin, who stood tall and proud, his armor gleaming in the sunlight.

"Take care, my friend," the Queen called out. "Watch over the Kingdom in my stead."

"I shall await your triumphant return, my Queen. Please do not take your time. Please hurry back," Svæin replied, his voice carrying across the courtyard. "May your sword be swift and your aim true."

Queen Valkyrja boarded her ship, setting sail towards the horizon as Ser Svæin watched her go, a silent guardian standing vigilant over the Kingdom in her absence. The fate of the Kingdom now rested in his hands, and he was prepared to defend it with his life.

Queen Valkyrja stood at the bow of her magnificent ship, her gaze fixed on the distant horizon. The wind whipped through her hair as she scanned the vast sea before her, determination etched into her features.

"Prepare the crew," she commanded, her voice carrying across the deck. "We sail for the land of Hrothgorn soldiers. We will show them the might of the Valkyrja warriors by vanquishing them on their own land."

As the crew bustled about, preparing for the perilous journey ahead, Queen Valkyrja retreated to her chambers to study maps and devise battle plans. Hours passed as she meticulously laid out strategies, her mind a whirlwind of tactics and possibilities. Finally satisfied, she emerged from her quarters, her eyes blazing with resolve.

"Gather 'round, warriors!" she called, her voice ringing out across the deck. "We shall strike at dawn. The Hrothgorn soldiers will regret the day they crossed paths with Queen Valkyrja and her fierce crew."

The crew listened intently as the Queen outlined her plans, each member hanging on her every word. The air crackled with anticipation, a sense of unity and purpose filling the ship.

One brave crewmember spoke, "Their numbers are vast, and their strength formidable. How shall we defeat them?"

Queen Valkyrja turned to face the young warrior, a steely glint in her eye. "We may be outnumbered, but we are Aromites! We fight with honor, courage, and skill. We will not falter in the face of adversity."

The crew cheered, their spirits lifted by their fearless leader's words. With hearts ablaze and swords at the ready, they awaited the break of dawn, ready to face whatever challenges awaited them.

As the first light of morning painted the sky in hues of pink and gold, Queen Valkyrja stood at the helm of her ship, her gaze fixed on the distant shore where the Hrothgorn soldiers awaited. Her voice rang out, strong and clear.

With a mighty roar, the Arcadia FrostWind surged forward, cutting through the waves towards their destiny. Queen Valkyrja and her crew sailed into battle, their spirits unbroken, and their resolve unshakable.

Artifact Nineteen

Dead Men's Sails

Date: Future Dimension of Höðr (2296 CE)
Near the Realm of the Panorama

"The grave will not eat before I have had my fill, damn you!"
-Dragonwulf

Shadows of Revenge

The void of space was not silent today. It hummed with the faint vibration of the mournful echoes of ships long lost in the deep. They seemed to weep in the depths of space. The Deepwater Watchman drifted on black currents of solar wind, her sails shimmering like the wings of a phantom. From the side, she looked much like the regal Lionfish of the Caribbean Sea.

"Captain," rasped his first mate, "we got a tail behind us. Crimson sails. She is running dark between the nebula tides. They mean to board us!"

"What flag does she fly?" asked Dragonwulf.

The first mate managed a strained answer, "It looks like a …claw. Maybe red, I think."

Dragonwulf's lip curled. "The Bloody Claw…Gladstone Grim!" He spoke the name like a curse, and yet there was an ache beneath it. Once, long ago, Grim had been his fiercest ally. It was Dragonwulf's old ship reworked and retooled for a new century. Grim had thrown him overboard and stolen his ship in the dead of the night many years ago. Dragonwulf always vowed revenge, harsh, bloody revenge. The Watchman angled into the Dark Void, a vast nebula cloud glowing red and gold, where ion storms could tear a ship apart. The Watchman's hull groaned as it cut through waves of crackling static.

Then she appeared, looming through the foggy mist, The Bloody Claw, red sails spread wide, and her bow was shaped like a beast's skull.

"Battle stations!" bellowed Dragonwulf. Cannons charged, grappling beams hummed, and the Watchman plunged directly at the Claw.

The two pirate ships clashed like beasts in the dark. Plasma fire ripped across space, the sails shredded, and crewmembers were hurled screaming into the abyss. The Watchman struck first blood, breaching the Claw's starboard hull, but her new Captain answered with a broadside of dark matter torpedoes that slammed into the Watchman's belly, tearing open decks like rotten wood.

Sparks showered down as the crew roared defiance. With a vicious grin, Dragonwulf gave the order. "Board her. Bring me Grim's filthy pirate head!"

The ships locked in a deadly embrace. Energy hooks bound iron to iron, and across the narrow bridges of fire and smoke, pirate met pirate.

Blades clashed. Steel collided with steel. Disruptors flared, and men screamed. Blood floated in zero gravity droplets.

At the heart of it, Dragonwulf and Grim met. Cutlass against a steel saber. Their duel rang like thunder across the decks.

"You betrayed me!" Dragonwulf snarled, sparks bursting as their blades clashed.

"That is not something you have done yourself to other Captains? Surely you do not think you are innocent!"

"After all these years, your mutiny stings like a knife wound to my backside! I believed you died many years ago!" said Dragonwulf.

"As they say, rumors of my death have been greatly exaggerated."

"Today you will pay for what you did!" said Dragonwulf

"No, I think not," Grim spat between his boots. "I just grew tired of you and your bloated stories."

The Watchman's engines bucked, tearing free of the Bloody Claw. The sudden lurch hurled them apart. Dragonwulf was dragged back to his ship, his blade lost, his pride wounded.

The two ships drifted in the nebula, crippled but not dead. The battle had no victor.

Dragonwulf stood on his battered deck, breathing hard, one hand pressed to his bleeding side. His crew looked to him with eyes of fire.

"She will try again," Old-Turas hissed.

Dragonwulf smiled, showing his teeth, sharp in the light.

"Aye, I hope so with all my being... And next time, I will end him."

The Deepwater Watchman limped into the dark, and the stars whispered of war.

The Ghost Fleet

The Deepwater Watchman floated wounded in the endless dark, sails torn, hull fractured, and engines coughing sparks. The crew labored to keep her alive, patching breaches with molten iron and welding new veins of power into her scarred bones.

Captain Old-Turas leaned uneasily upon the quarterdeck, his eyes burning as he studied the drifting debris from their last clash. There were bits of crimson sail and shards of iron bone from The Bloody Claw.

"I do not think I need to remind you, old pirate, that this is not why we are out here to begin with," said Old-Turas to a wounded Dragonwulf. "We are on the hunt for the Defiler of Souls. Not Gladstone Grim."

"We can do both! I refuse to let Grim slip through my hands. I must have him," said a stubborn Dragonwulf. "I must see him bleed and suffer."

"She will be hunting us anyway," rasped Luciano Cantore. "I would not give up if *I were them.*"

"Aye," Dragonwulf muttered. "Gladstone Grim is as relentless as the tide. We will see him bleed from the yardarm! Then we will resume the course. The defiler scratches his way through the universe, and we must stop him.

Before he could say more, a sound shimmered across the comm-lines. It was an encoded frequency, old as the void itself. A whispering call barely audible above the static of the airwaves.

"Cap," said the helmsman, pale and wide-eyed, "you will want to hear this."

The signal crackled through the ship's ancient radio. It was faint, broken, as if it had traveled centuries to reach them.

"…ghosts… fleet… riches beyond the suns… the lost Armada…"

Dragonwulf's blood ran hot. The Ghost Fleet was a legend whispered in every port since he was a cabin boy. A thousand warships are said to drift in eternal silence, their holds bursting with plunder and weapons beyond imagination.

"Mark the coordinates," Captain Old-Turas growled. "Set course."

"What about our mission, you old goat?" asked Dragonwulf. "It is quite different when it applies to treasure and weapons."

"Shut your gob and pilot this bucket of splinters. I will go below and let the crew know what we are doing. The Defiler can wait a day."

Dragonwulf hoped to persuade the Destiny of Tyr to deviate from the voyage to make repairs.

In the dark between the stars, beyond the nebula, another ship listened.

The Bloody Claw, battered but alive, prowled like a hungry beast.

On her bridge, Gladstone Grim leaned against his wheel, still bloodied and wounded, and had caught the signal.

"The Ghost Fleet," he murmured. "Of course, Dragonwulf will chase it."

His quartermaster tilted his head. "Shall we follow, Captain?"

Grim's lips curved in a cruel smile. "Not *follow*, quartermaster, we will *hunt*. The Watchman will lead us straight to the prize, and then, I will take it from her bones."

⎯⎯⎯⎯⎯⎯

The journey carried them into the Captain's Den, a graveyard of shattered dreams and drifting wrecks. A cemetery of broken and ancient ships floated like corpses, their sails long burned to ash.

On the Bloody Claw, the crew whispered of curses. Men swore they saw shadows moving across the deck when no one stood there.

"Captain," the first mate bellowed, slamming a fist against the bulkhead, "this place is wrong. There are spirits here. No treasure is worth your soul. I can feel their evil spirits from here, Captain!"

Grim stared into the expanse, his one living eye narrowed. "Good. Then it means we are close."

They moved without engines, without crew, drifting as though alive. Their lights burned faint and cold.

The Claw's crew fell silent, awe and terror mingling.

Grim's smile was wicked. "Arm the hooks. We take what we can before Old-Turas and Deepwater arrive."

The Ghost Fleet drifted like men slain and left to rot. A thousand warships, their sails vast as the sea, glided silently through the Captain's Den. Some were cracked in half, spilling their bones of iron. Others gleamed as if new-forged, untouched by time.

On the Bloody Claw, the crew gathered at the rails, staring with wide eyes. Even hardened cutthroats trembled at the sight.

"Dead men's sails," muttered the first mate. "They've waited centuries, Captain. "What is their reason for this?"

"The only reason is plunder. Those holds are heavy with relics. Enough treasure to buy ten galaxies."

The Claw crept closer to the nearest hulk, grappling beams lashing out, locking onto the ghost ship's ribs.

"Boarding party," Grim ordered. "First blood's ours."

The Claw's raiders stepped into the ancient vessel. Silence swallowed them. The air smelled of rust and grave-dust. Their boots echoed down corridors lined with banners stiff as bone.

"Empty," whispered one of the crew. "All hands have gone to dust."

As they passed the central hall, torches flared to life. Not torches of fire—torches of plasma, burning in colors no living eye had seen.

From the shadows stepped figures clad in armor blackened by ages. Their faces were skulls, their sockets glowing with cold starlight. The Dead Fleet still had its crew.

Blades rang free. Gunfire cracked. Screams echoed as the Claw's crew met the risen dead in brutal combat. Disruptors and plasma guns burned holes through bone, but the skeletons fought without pain, without fear. Ancient sabers clashed against plasma cutlasses, sparks showering the silent hall.

Grim himself waded into the fray, his cutlass crackling. He split one skull in half, and then another, grinning as bone dust clouded the air. "That is the damn shame about killing your enemies. You cannot kill them twice! You cannot kill what is already dead," he snarled.

A booming voice rolled through the ship, shaking the iron bones of its hull:

"Who dares plunder the armada of the eternal?"

The air itself trembled. The crew faltered. Grim's smile widened.

"I dare," he said, lifting his blade as he recognized the figure of Dragonwulf.

Then the Deepwater Watchman struck.

Wolfclaw's ship locked its grappling beams into the ghost vessel's other flank, her raiders swarming aboard. Crimson sails glowed outside the shattered hull as her boarding party swept in, blasting bone and pirate alike.

Dragonwulf walked through the smoke, saber gleaming red. He locked eyes with Grim across the chaos.

"Still alive, then?" he called, his voice cutting above the din. "I thought the dead would have swallowed you whole by now."

"I am still a better pirate than you," Grim spat between his boots yet again. "Even the grave won't feed before I've had my fill!"

The two crews clashed, pirate against pirate, even as the dead empire pressed in around them. The dead ship became a storm of blades, bullets, and bone.

Larger than both pirate ships combined, the flagship's hull was a jagged mausoleum of black steel and bone-like spires, lit by veins of sickly green fire. Every sensor aboard both ships screamed in warning, and every living soul felt the sudden cold that seeped into their bones.

"Mortals, your petty quarrel trespasses upon sacred ground," warned the Admiral of the fleet.

The Armada of the Dead, a legion of forgotten captains and cursed crews bound to eternal slumber, now stirred.

The Admiral's voice deepened, dripping with rage.

"You have awakened them. The armada will not suffer your bickering. Leave... or be drawn into their ranks."

On the bridges of The Deepwater Watchman and The Bloody Claw, hardened pirates who had faced death a thousand times now found their hands trembling. Their quarrel seemed suddenly small in the presence of the endless ghost fleet. The captains exchanged a single glance across the void. Fear coiled in their bellies, but neither was ready to surrender.

The Armada of the Dead stirred like a nest of serpents.

The Armada's Admiral stretched its colossal wings of metal and shadow, and its voice thundered across the void.

The two pirate captains, once bitter enemies, opened a channel across the open space, their voices raw with defiance.

"We will die if we fight each other."

"Then let us give the dead something to choke on!"

The Deepwater Watchman and The Bloody Claw burned as they fought, hulls torn open, oxygen venting in geysers of flame and ice. They surged forward, engines screaming, guns hot, and defiance holding them together when steel alone could not.

The Armada of the Dead closed in around them, a tightening noose of wraith-like ships. Every blast of pirate cannon tore through ghostly hulls, only for the fallen to rise again,

At the center of it all, in place of the ghost Admiral, was *the face of the Defiler of Souls.*

"Board it," growled Captain Old Turas with blood dripping down his scarred face. "Is this not what we came for?"

"The Defiler just handed himself over to us!" said Dragonwulf.

Captain Grim spat back, "You mad bastard! Let us give the devil his due."

The two pirate ships broke formation, thrusters roaring. With shields gone and hulls failing, they hurled themselves directly into the ghost ship's shadow.

Both ships slammed grappling harpoons into the Defiler's black hull. Metal shrieked, sparks showered, and then hatches blew open. All at once through the gaping hatches, they peered into the darkness, and it emerged in its hellish glory. The Götterdämmerung appeared like a demon ghost in the darkness. Hundreds of pirates—cutthroats, killers, survivors all—spilled into the nightmare corridors of the Defiler of Souls through the open gangways.

"What do we do now?" asked Captain Grim.

"I do not know," answered Dragonwulf. "I have never been this close to it."

Inside, the air was colder than death. The walls pulsed like veins. Shadows twisted into shapes of long-dead men, whispering, clawing, and laughing. Crewmembers fell screaming as their souls were ripped from their bodies, but others pressed on, blades and plasma rifles blazing, cutting their way deeper into the beast.

A churning black sphere was the holding place for souls. The screams of a million souls emitted from the void of the sphere.

"Fools! You cannot kill death," hissed the Defiler.

"We do not have to kill you," said Dragonwulf. Show your face to me! We just have to return you to the Council of Gods for your punishment. I *will* kill you if I am forced to. Give me a reason.

Unknown to Dragonwulf, Captain Grim had set a plasma detonation that ripped the Armada of the dead apart in a wave of screaming fire. Ghost ships disintegrated into dust and ash, and a million souls scattered like sparks across the stars.

They had destroyed the Ghost Armada, and all that remained was the Defiler of Souls and the Gotterdammerung unscathed.

The Defiler deposited both Captains on their ships with their crews.

"Come back and face me! You coward! Have you no stomach for the fight/" he bellowed to the Defiler.

A faint whisper lingered, and a solemn promise was uttered.

"I will return. We will meet again soon enough. You did not think it was going to be that easy, did you?"

The wreckage of the battle drifted for days. Shattered hulls, broken weapons, frozen corpses—an entire graveyard of pirate fury and undead wrath.

The Armada of the Dead, The *Defiler of Souls*, and the charge into the belly of the beast, and it was all done in one day. The two brave Captains who breached the Planet killer decided to go their separate ways, no longer to seek revenge upon each other. There was a much bigger fight in store.

Artifact Nineteen

The Phantom of the Sea

Dimension of Óðinn (126 AD)

"I wish that time would freeze in place and the gods would forget about me and go about their business. I have no wish for the passage of time."
-Captain Old Turas

Upon the deck of her majestic ship, The Arcadia Frost-Wind Queen Valkyrja fixed her sights on the snow-capped peaks of the Winterhawk Mountains in the distance. Beside her, her loyal band of warriors prepared for the treacherous journey ahead. They had pursued King Draknorr's Hrothgorn warriors into the sea and beyond.

"Prepare you, my brave companions," Queen Valkyrja proclaimed, her voice carrying across the deck. "We pursue the vile Hrothgorn into the heart of the Winterhawk Mountains. We will not rest until justice is served and the land is rid of his evil."

The crew cheered in response, their spirits lifted by their queen's unwavering determination. As The Arcadia sliced through the icy waters, Queen Valkyrja's thoughts turned to the sea phantom, a mysterious being said to possess ancient wisdom that could aid her in her quest.

Days turned into weeks as the ship sailed ever closer to the towering mountains. Finally, they reached the shores of the Winterhawk, a desolate and unforgiving land where only the bravest dared to tread. Queen Valkyrja disembarked, sword in hand, her heart filled with both fear and resolve.

As she ventured deeper into the mountains, the wind howled, and the snow fell around her like a swirling maelstrom. Suddenly, a figure appeared before her - the sea phantom, its form ethereal and shimmering.

"Queen Valkyrja, ruler of the seas," the sea phantom's voice echoed in her mind. "I have long awaited your arrival. The path ahead is perilous, but fear not, for I shall impart upon you the wisdom you seek."

"Tell me what I must know, Phantom of the Sea."

The phantom nodded slowly, its ethereal form shimmering in the mist. "Very well, brave queen. Always remember, true strength lies not just in battles fought but also in the wisdom to choose the right path. Seek out the ancient oracle of the Winterhawk, for only she can show you the way to victory.

Queen Valkyrja listened intently as the sea phantom spoke of sacrifice and courage, of loyalty and honor. The wisdom flowed through her like a warm breeze, filling her with a newfound strength and clarity.

The Winterhawk

Long before Dragonwulf drew breath as a man, before his name was carved into steel and sung by dying warriors, the Winterhawk was chosen.

She was not born beneath a sun, but beneath a sky of ash and falling snow, in the farthest reaches of the North where even the gods spoke in whispers. The Old Ones called that place *Skarnfell*, the last place where fate could still be read in the wind. It was there that the **Destiny of Tyr** unfolded a single command:

Follow the Wolf. Do not guide his hand. Do not shield his heart. Only watch—and remember.

The Winterhawk was once mortal. His true name has been lost to time, spoken now only by the dead. She was a soldier of uncommon restraint, never the first to strike, never the last to flee. Where others burned with glory, he endured. Tyr marked her not for his strength, but for his stillness.

When Dragonwulf was born, reborn, and reborn again across ages and wars, the Winterhawk followed.

He walked as a hunter, a healer, a monk, a nameless man at the edge of the battlefield. At times, he was near enough to hear his breath as he slept; at others, separated by oceans and centuries. He never spoke to him of fate. Never warned him. Never praised him. The Destiny of Tyr forbade it. His role was not to shape the path but to ensure the path was remembered exactly as it unfolded.

As Dragonwulf died and returned, the Winterhawk changed. At times, he was a brave warrior, and other times, she became a wise sage.

His hair whitened and never darkened again. His eyes took on the pale, reflective hue of ice under moonlight. Ravens ceased to circle him; hawks did not. Winter followed his steps, not as cold, but as silence. He learned the language of snow, the truth hidden in frost, the way time slows in the presence of inevitability.

It was during the time of the *Twilight of the Gods* that he ceased to age altogether.

The Phantom of the Sea, older than storms, older than sails, rose from the black water and named him what he had become.

"You are no longer a watcher alone," the Phantom intoned. *"You are the oracle."*

From that moment, the Winterhawk became not one who foretells futures, but one who reveals what must be understood. He does not speak in riddles to obscure truth, but in truths so cold and sharp they must be handled with care.

His sanctuary formed naturally, as all true oracles do.

And now, the Queen comes.

The Phantom of the Sea has sent her—not to ask how to win, but to ask how to endure what must be lost.

The Winterhawk knows this Queen will not leave unchanged.

He has watched Dragonwulf all his days—watched him rage, love, fail, rise, and shatter heaven itself. He knows what price fate demands of rulers who stand too close to him. He knows what crowns cost when destiny tightens its grip.

The Queen kneels before *him,* but the Winterhawk will not bow.

He will spread his pale mantle like frost across the stone and speak not as servant, nor prophet, but as witness.

And for the first time since Tyr marked him, the Destiny will allow him to do more than watch.

He will impart wisdom not to change Dragonwulf's path, but to ensure the Queen survives walking beside it.

Queen Valkyrja, with her heart of steel and eyes of ice, reached the Mountain of the Winterhawk. It loomed in the distance, its peak shrouded in mist and mystery. As she made her way through the snowy terrain, her loyal companions, the valiant knights of Arom, rode alongside her.

Upon reaching the base of the mountain, Queen Valkyrja gazed up in awe at the sheer magnitude of the Winterhawk's domain. The wind howled through the cracks and crevices, carrying with it the whisper of ancient magic. With determination etched on her face, she began the treacherous ascent.

After hours of climbing, Queen Valkyrja and her knights finally reached the summit. There, perched majestically on a ledge, sat the Winterhawk, a creature of legend and myth. His feathers gleamed with an otherworldly light, and his piercing gaze bore into the Queen's soul.

"Who entreats upon my domain?" the Winterhawk's voice echoed through the mountain, sending shivers down the spines of all who heard it.

"I am Queen Valkyrja of Arom, and I seek your wisdom, great Winterhawk," the Queen replied, her voice steady despite the awe that filled her heart." We have already had the pleasure of meeting you as you accompanied our hero Wolfclaw Dragonwülf to the halls of Valhalla."

"I followed that brave soul all the days of his life only to serve him. He was taken from me by the Destiny of Tyr."

"We seek your help, mighty Winterhawk. We must stop the threat of the Hrothgorn against the Kingdom of Arom so we can help Dragonwülf and the Destiny of Tyr stop The Defiler."

"I pursued him throughout the realm and lost him many years ago in the Kingdom of DragonBorne," said the Winterhawk in a morose tone.

"So you are familiar with the beast, Defiler?" asked the Queen.

"Yes... he was responsible for the death of some of my brothers and sisters. I thought I would never get another chance to find him. Allow me the honor of joining you in your quest.

"I would consider it an honor and a blessing from the gods that we might have the great and mighty Winterhawk with us on our quest," said Queen Valkyrja.

The Ambush at Mountain Pass

Queen Valkyrja and her army marched through the treacherous mountain pass, the snow crunching beneath their boots as they pressed forward. The Winterhawk watched from high above. They were on their way to reinforce their allies in the neighboring kingdom, unaware of the danger lurking ahead.

As they rounded a bend, the tranquility of the pass was shattered as a deafening roar echoed through the icy air. Before they could react, a hail of arrows rained down on them from the cliffs above, taking out several soldiers in an instant.

"Take cover!" Queen Valkyrja's commanding voice rang out as she raised her shield, deflecting an arrow just in time. The sounds of battle erupted all around them as her army scrambled for shelter.

"Where are they coming from?" demanded one of the soldiers, panic evident in his voice.

"Up there, on the cliffs!" another soldier yelled, pointing towards the shadowy figures raining death upon them.

Queen Valkyrja's eyes narrowed as she scanned the cliffs, her mind working quickly. "We must take out their vantage points. Archers, come with me!" she ordered, leading a small group towards the rocky incline.

As they climbed, arrows whistled past them, narrowly missing their heads. The Queen's heart pounded with adrenaline as she reached the enemy archers, engaging them in fierce combat.

"Come to us and let us kill you humanely! Make us chase you, and you will suffer needlessly." Hrothgorn General Kor taunted, swinging his sword wildly.

"Come and see what will befall you, foolhardy Hrothgorn!" taunted The Queen.

The adversaries rushed toward each other in a fury of steel and blood. The Queen spread the full array of her wings in full view of the enemy and her own Knights.

The icy winds howled through the barren landscape as Queen Valkyrja and her army rushed towards the Northern army to face the Hrothgorn of the Northlands in a battle that would determine the fate of their kingdoms. The ground was covered in a thick blanket of snow, the air cold and biting, but the determination in Valkyrja's eyes burned fiercely.

As the two armies stood facing each other across the frozen valley, the tension in the air was palpable. The Hrothgorn, massive warriors adorned in fur and wielding mighty axes, let out thunderous roars that echoed through the mountains.

"You dare to challenge me, Queen Valkyrja?" General Kor bellowed, his voice carrying the weight of years of conquest and battle. "Prepare to meet your end at the hands of the Northlands!"

Valkyrja, her sword gleaming in the pale light, raised her head high and met his gaze without flinching. "I will not back down, Hrothgorn. Your tyranny ends here and now."

With a wordless cry, the two armies clashed in a fury of steel and blood. Valkyrja fought with the skill of a seasoned warrior, her movements graceful yet deadly. The Hrothgorn swung his axe with brute force, each blow shaking the ground beneath them.

"Your people will bow before me, Valkyrja!" he roared, his eyes filled with malice.

Nevertheless, Valkyrja was undaunted. "We will never surrender to one such as you, Kor. Our freedom is our strength!"

The battle raged on, the clash of weapons and cries of the fallen filling the air. As the sun began to sink below the horizon, both leaders found themselves locked in a fierce duel at the edge of a cliff overlooking the valley.

"You fight well, Queen Valkyrja," Kor grunted, his breath heavy with exertion. "But it ends here. You will fall before me."

Valkyrja smiled grimly, her eyes flashing with determination. "I will not fall, Hrothgorn. I will rise, like the phoenix from the ashes."

With a sudden burst of speed, she unleashed a series of lightning-fast strikes, each one finding its mark with deadly accuracy. The Hrothgorn stumbled back, a look of shock crossing his face as he realized he had been outmatched. Behind the Queen stood four Hrothgorn warriors with raised square hammers, converging on her.

They bellowed "Mat Gorna Mat Murna!"

"Kill Hrothgorn heroes. Slay with much haste."

As they swung their hammers toward the Queen's head, the Winterhawk swooped down from above and violently grasped the Hrothgorn soldier two in each taloned claw. She flew high above the forest as they screamed and writhed, and then dropped them in the stony canyon below the cliffs, breaking them to pieces.

The Queen was able to finish her battle with General Kor after the intervention of the Winterhawk.

"It... it cannot be," Kor gasped, his grip on his axe faltering.

Valkyrja seized the opportunity, her final blow striking true and sending General Kor tumbling over the edge of the cliff. As his form disappeared into the darkness below, a hush fell over the battlefield.

Kor's soldiers fought on.

"You have no leader, you fools!" cried the Queen. The clash of steel against steel echoed through the pass as the warriors fought, each refusing to give an inch. The queen's army, inspired by her bravery, pushed back against the ambushers with renewed vigor.

"Take them down, for the Queen!" a soldier shouted, rallying his comrades as they charged into the fray.

Amidst the chaos and the clash of swords, Queen Valkyrja's voice rose above the fray, unwavering and fierce. "We fight not just for ourselves, but for the future of our kingdom!"

As the sun dipped below the horizon, casting a warm glow over the snow-covered pass, the last of the enemy forces retreated, defeated by the bravery and unity of Queen Valkyrja and her army.

Exhausted but victorious, Queen Valkyrja stood amid the fallen, her gaze steely and unwavering. "We may have won this battle, but the war is far from over. We must remain vigilant, for our enemies will stop at nothing to see us fall."

Artifact Twenty

The Gunslinger and the Actor

Dimension of Frigg 1865 CE, Arizona Territory, Earth

"Is it strange that I miss a place where I ain't ever been? I feel like I'm at home thinking about some forest somewhere, and I don't know anything about it."
-Zachariah Boyd.

The Deepwater Watchman, Dragonwülf, and its crew passed the historical window of the Old West and the timeline of April 1865, and gunslinger Zachariah Boyd. As if shot from a sling, Boyd found himself hurtling through space and time.

Amidst the rugged terrain of the Wild West, the cowboy rode his horse through the desolate canyons, the sound of his faithful steed's hooves echoing against the red rock walls. The sun dipped below the horizon, casting long shadows across the land as Boyd pressed forward, his eyes scanning the horizon for any signs of danger. Suddenly, a haunting sound pierced the stillness of the evening - the mournful howl of hounds in the distance. Boyd's heart quickened as he recognized the sound, knowing all too well what it meant.

"You hear the hounds' wailing," Boyd muttered to his horse, urging him to pick up the pace. "The mountains groan out a sad song."

The lone rider galloped into the small town of Dusty Creek as the sun dipped below the horizon, casting long shadows over the dusty streets. The townspeople whispered amongst themselves, their eyes following the mysterious stranger as he made his way to the local saloon.

"He's back in town," a grizzled old man muttered to his companion, his hands trembling as he reached for his whiskey.

Boyd dismounted his horse with an air of quiet confidence, his weathered face set in a steely gaze as he surveyed the crowded saloon. The piano music faltered, and the room fell silent as all eyes turned to the dangerous man in their midst.

"What can I get for ya, stranger?" the barkeep asked, his voice tinged with nervousness.

Boyd's eyes swept over the room before finally settling on the barkeep. "Whiskey," he said.

As the barkeep poured him a drink, a young woman approached the cowboy cautiously.

"You're Boyd, ain't ya?" she asked, her voice shaking slightly.

He nodded, taking a long swig of his whiskey before answering. "That's what they call me."

The woman bit her lip, her eyes darting around the room. "They say you're trouble," she said, her voice barely above a whisper. "I like trouble, mister."

He chuckled darkly, the sound sending shivers down the spines of those around him. "Trouble finds me, darlin'. I just make sure it never catches up to me."

Just then, the swinging doors of the saloon burst open, and a group of rough-looking men spilled inside, their hands hovering over their holstered guns. "Well, as I live and breathe and stand downwind, if it ain't Zach Boyd. I thought I smelled you," one of them sneered.

Boyd's hand drifted to the gun strapped to his hip, his eyes narrowing as he regarded the newcomers. "Looking for trouble, boys?"

The leader of the group stepped forward, a cruel smile playing on his lips. "We heard you were back in town. Figured we'd come to say howdy."

A tense silence filled the room as the standoff unfolded, the townspeople holding their breath in anticipation of the impending violence. Boyd's hand twitched, and in a flash, his gun was drawn and aimed at the leader's head.

"Say howdy, then," said the cowboy.

The leader hesitated for a moment before slowly backing away, his companions following suit. With a satisfied smirk, Boyd holstered his gun and drained the last of his whiskey.

"Remember my new name, boys," he called after them, his voice a warning in the stillness of the saloon. "Y'all can call me Sundown, and I'll be seeing you."

Later on a fateful day in 1855, Zachariah Boyd rode into another town on his trusty steed, a glint of determination in his steely eyes. He had an appointment with destiny here.

As the sun began to set, casting an orange glow over the town, Zachariah made his way to the local saloon. The swinging doors creaked as he pushed them open, the chatter inside dying down as all eyes turned to him. The atmosphere was tense, but his gaze never wavered as he made his way to the poker table at the back of the room.

Seated at the table were three figures, unlike any Boyd had ever encountered. Their skin was a sickly shade of green, their eyes glowing with an otherworldly light. Zachariah knew immediately that these were no ordinary card players - they were demons.

Despite their eerie presence, Boyd took a seat at the table, his hand hovering over his holster. The demons regarded him with a mix of amusement and curiosity as if they knew the secrets he held.

The game began, the cards sliding smoothly across the worn table as tension mounted with each hand. The first demon, Ozymandias, slicked back his obsidian hair and leered at the gunslinger with a grin that promised pain.

"Tell me, gunslinger," he crooned, his voice as smooth as silk and as sharp as a dagger. "What brings a mortal like you to a place like this?"

The gunslinger kept his gaze steady as he replied, "I'm here for the same reason as anyone else. I want to try my luck at the table." "A foolish endeavor," scoffed the second demon,

Lilith spoke, her voice like a whisper in the dark, "Luck means nothing in a game such as this. It is skill, cunning, and a willingness to embrace the darkness that will see you through."

The gunslinger chuckled, the sound grating against the ears of those who heard it. "I've faced my fair share of darkness in my time," he said, his hand hovering over the revolver at his side. "I'm not afraid to do what needs to be done."

The third demon let out a guttural laugh that shook the very foundations of the room. "Ah, but what if what needs to be done is more than you can handle?" he growled, his eyes gleaming with malice. "What then? Will you still be so brave in the face of true darkness?"

The gunslinger's hand tightened around the hilt of his gun, his jaw set in a defiant line. "I have faced demons far worse than you three," he said, his voice laced with a steely resolve. "I ain't got the powers you got, but I have something you don't - a soul that ain't ever been to hell. No matter, I am here today lookin' for someone you are hidin'."

"Who might that be, you dusty road traveler?" asked Lilith

"You know who I am talkin' about, you fork-toothed liar," said Boyd.

As the night wore on, the young cowboy's skills were put to the test. The demons seemed to know his every move before he made it, their supernatural abilities giving them an edge in the game. Nevertheless, Boyd was determined. He knew that the fate of the future rested on his shoulders, and he would not be swayed.

Finally, as the clock struck midnight, he laid down his winning hand - a royal flush that would seal his victory. The demons' faces twisted in rage, their forms flickering like shadows in the candlelight. However, Boyd was ready. With lightning speed, he drew his revolver and aimed it at the demons, his finger tightening on the trigger.

"Where is John Wilkes Booth?" he demanded, his voice cutting through the tense silence of the saloon. The demons sneered, their voices echoing with a chilling resonance. "My hand defeated your scaly hands today. I am triumphant! You *will* tell me what I need to know! Now, where is Booth?"

"He is beyond your reach, gunslinger," they hissed. "Why do you want him so badly?" asked one of the demons.

"I think you *slobber-lipped liars* know exactly what he plans, and I'm here to stop him," answered Boyd. "You also know that the last time I was here, I killed a man during a card game, and *I hung fer it*. Show me where Booth is, you filthy demons," said Boyd as he squeezed off a shot at one of their heads. They vanished before Boyd's bullet crossed the room.

Just then, in the dimly lit saloon at the vanishing point of the demons, the sound of shuffling cards filled the room as a renowned actor entered, ordered a drink, and sat at a table, engaged in a game of poker with a group of rowdy men. John Wilkes Booth's charismatic smile and confident demeanor were unmistakable as he cleverly played his hand, charming the onlookers with his wit and skill.

As the game progressed, the atmosphere grew tense when Boyd locked eyes with Booth, his expression unreadable.

"Care to join us for a poker hand, stranger?" Booth called out, flashing a charming grin as he gestured to an empty seat at the table.

Boyd slowly made his way over, his every step deliberate and calculated. Without a word, he placed a revolver on the table, the gleam of its barrel catching the dim light of the saloon.

"I ain't here for cards, Booth. I'm here to put an end to your plans," Boyd said, his voice low and menacing.

Booth's grin faltered, his eyes narrowing in suspicion. "What plans would they be, my friend?" he asked, attempting to mask the unease in his voice.

"You plan to assassinate President Lincoln at Ford's Theatre later this month on the 14th, but I aim to stop you before you can pull that trigger," Boyd declared, his hand hovering over the grip of his gun.

The other patrons in the saloon watched on as the tension in the air thickened with each passing moment.

Booth's gaze hardened as he rose from his seat, his thespian charm giving way to steely resolve. "You have no proof of such accusations, stranger. I suggest you leave before you make a *grave* mistake," he warned, his hand inching towards his own concealed weapon.

Boyd's eyes remained fixed on Booth, his resolve unwavering. "I don't need any proof to know a man's intentions, Booth. I can see it in your eyes," he said, his voice cold and unyielding. "I know that you're one of them fancy dandies, but you got somethin' really wrong with you."

"What might you be getting at, young man?" asked Booth.

Boyd's gaze remained unwavering. "I could ask you the same, Booth. What devil's business are you up to?"

A flicker of surprise crossed Booth's features before it was replaced by a sly grin. "Just a bit of theatrics, my friend, but nothing that concerns you."

Boyd could sense the undercurrent of deceit in Booth's words. His instincts, honed by years of survival in the unforgiving West, screamed a warning. "I've heard whispers of your latest performance, Booth. The stage you're planning isn't fit for civilized folk."

Booth's mask slipped for a moment, his eyes flashing with annoyance before he regained his composure. "You underestimate me, Boyd. My vision transcends your narrow view of the world."

"I hear you've been making some bold moves, Booth. Are ya plannin' a big performance? Do ya care to fill me in?"

Booth's smile widened a glint of mischief in his eyes. "Just a little grand finale, you might say."

Boyd's hand drifted towards the handle of his revolver, his expression hardening. "I don't like being kept in the dark, Booth. What's this grand finale of yours all about?"

Booth leaned in, his voice dropping to a whisper.

"I plan to rid this country of its greatest menace for the last time. Then I will take my curtain call."

Boyd's eyes narrowed, a mix of disbelief and fury flashing across his face. "You're talking about Lincoln. You want to kill the President?"

Booth chuckled, a chilling sound that sent shivers down Boyd's spine. "Are you going to stand in my way? You are a colossal charlatan! You kill men without a second thought, but heaven forbid I have the best interests of my beloved country at heart. Do you assume you will stay my hand, boy?"

Boyd's hand tightened around his revolver, his voice deadly quiet. "I reckon I just might. You see, Booth, I might be a killer, but I ain't no traitor. You, Sir, are walking a dangerous line."

The tension in the air was palpable as the two men locked eyes, each sizing up the other. At that moment, a silent understanding passed between them - a realization that they were bound by a code, even if their paths diverged.

Booth finally broke the stare, a ghost of a smile playing on his lips.

"Well, well, it seems we're at an impasse, Boyd. Perhaps we'll meet again on opposite sides of history."

"Your path ends here, Booth," said Boyd.

With a sudden movement, Booth reached for the concealed weapon at his side, but Boyd was faster. In a blur of motion, the room erupted in chaos as gunfire echoed through the saloon. When the smoke cleared, Booth lay on the floor, his once-charming face twisted in anger and disbelief.

Boyd stood over him, the weight of his actions heavy in his heart. "You chose your fate, Booth. May God have mercy on your soul."

Boyd stood victorious, his gun still smoking as he gazed down at the fallen figure of John Wilkes Booth. The assassin was stopped by a simple man known as Sundown.

Artifact Twenty-One

Sic Semper Tyrannis!

Dimension of Frigg 1865 CE
Washington, DC, Earth

"One who would win a war is a warrior most exquisite; one who prevents war flies with the angels forever.

- President Abraham Lincoln, 1925 CE

Boyd wiped the sweat from his brow as he surveyed the dusty town, his hand gripping the hilt of his gun. The notorious gunslinger had been called upon by the Destiny of Tyr to kill the future assassin of President Abraham Lincoln. He was joined now by Dragonwülf beside him with his battle-axe at the ready.

"I reckon we've done our part," Zach said, squinting against the sun.

In the dark realm of the supernatural, where treachery and deceit reign supreme, the demon Ozymandias saw an opportunity to fulfill his craving for chaos and destruction. He set his sights on the mortal realm, where a great man, Abraham Lincoln, stood as a beacon of hope and unity.

"John, my faithful Servant," Ozymandias hissed, appearing before the simple grave of John Wilkes Booth. "I have a task for you, one that will secure your place in history and wreak havoc on the mortals." The ground beneath quivered and caved inward, forcing the demon to jump to one side. Rising from the dirt and mud was the corpse of the assassin.

Booth stood upright, his eyes filled with malice and desperation, listening intently to the demon's sinister plan. Dirt and mud fell from his face and hair. It was a far departure from the most famous actor in America.

"What is it that you require of me?" he asked, his voice tainted with bitterness.

"You shall be the instrument of Lincoln's demise," Ozymandias declared, his voice dripping with malevolence. "But not through the means of your failed assassination. No, we shall orchestrate a grander scheme that will plunge the mortal realm into chaos."

Booth's eyes widened with a mixture of confusion and intrigue. "Tell me more," he urged, a flicker of hope igniting within him. "I have already paid with my life for my plot to do just that. A young gunslinger put me in this filthy grave," he said with a low voice just above a whisper.

Ozymandias whispered dark secrets and twisted lies into Booth's mind, weaving a web of deceit that would lead the mortal to believe he held the power to alter history itself. The demon's words enveloped Booth like a shroud, clouding his judgment and fueling his desire for revenge.

As the night fell over the mortal realm, Booth, guided by the demon's whispered promises, set his plan into motion.

In the dimly lit theater, President Abraham Lincoln sat watching the play "Our American Cousin" with his wife, Mary. The atmosphere was filled with excitement and laughter as the actors delivered their lines with passion.

"You have caused great pain and suffering, Lincoln," Booth sneered, his eyes ablaze with a twisted sense of righteousness. "Now, it is time for you to pay the ultimate price for your sins."

Lincoln, ever the embodiment of wisdom and compassion, regarded Booth with a mixture of sorrow and understanding. "I sense darkness within you, John," he said, his voice calm yet resolute. "But know this, violence and hatred shall never triumph over unity and love."

As Booth raised his weapon, fueled by the demon's whispers and his own misguided sense of justice, a blinding light engulfed the scene. Ozymandias materialized before them, his form towering and wraithlike.

"John, you have been deceived," the demon spoke, his voice booming with cruel laughter. "You were but a pawn in my grand design, a mere tool for chaos and destruction."

Booth, his eyes widening with a mixture of horror and realization, fell to his knees, his weapon clattering to the ground. "No, this cannot be," he whispered, his soul consumed by regret and guilt.

As Ozymandias unleashed his true power, the mortal realm quaked with the force of his wrath. Abraham Lincoln, standing resolute in the face of darkness, faced the demon with unwavering courage.

"You may seek to sow chaos and destruction, demon," Lincoln declared, his voice unwavering. "But know this: the light of hope shall never be extinguished."

The realms of mortals and demons clashed in a tumultuous dance of power and will. A gunshot echoed through the theater, causing everyone to freeze in shock.

John Wilkes Booth, a famous actor and Confederate sympathizer possessed by the spirit of the demon Ozymandias, had just shot the President. Chaos ensued as the audience realized what had happened. Mrs. Lincoln screamed in horror while Booth leaped onto the stage, shouting, "Sic semper tyrannis!" before fleeing into the night.

The wounded President was quickly carried to a nearby house where doctors did their best to save him, but the bullet had lodged deep in his brain, and nothing could save him. As Lincoln lay on his deathbed, he whispered his final words to his wife, expressing his love for her and his hopes for the future of their country.

"Please, Mary, do not let it end here," the President pleaded.

Meanwhile, a massive manhunt was underway to capture John Wilkes Booth. He would not be found. Ozymandias hissed, "They search for a dead man and deny the existence of gods and demons! Damned Fools!"

The nation mourned the loss of its beloved President, a man who had led it through the Civil War and towards the abolition of slavery. His assassination sent shockwaves around the world, leaving a legacy of courage, compassion, and unity in its wake.

As the curtains closed on that fateful night at Ford's Theater, the echoes of the gunshot lingered in the minds of a nation forever changed by the actions of a dead man driven by hate and misguided beliefs. As the angels accompanied the President on his new journey, they sang a new song.

"When the wicked return, taking a new form,
Surrender the spirit to a vessel that is warm.
To one with a pure heart who has braved the storm,
He gave birth to a new age at the break of dawn."

In the heart of a secluded forest, the Destiny of Tyr gathered around a flickering campfire. Abraham Lincoln stood in awe as the blinding light enveloped him, transporting him to the deck of the Deepwater Watchman. Before him were the Destiny of Tyr and the crew of the ship of heroes. Avat'or spoke in a voice that resonated through Lincoln's very being.

"We are the Destiny of Tyr," the alien intoned, "and we seek your assistance, Abraham Lincoln."

The former president's mind raced with confusion and wonder. "What do you want from me?" he managed to ask.

"We offer you resurrection, Mr. Lincoln," Avat'or replied, his voice soothing yet filled with power. "In return, we ask for your Service to the Destiny of Tyr."

Lincoln's heart swelled with conflicting emotions. The chance to live again, to make amends for his unfinished work, was a temptation beyond measure. To leave behind everything he knew and loved on Earth was a decision of cosmic proportions.

After a moment of contemplation, Lincoln nodded solemnly. "I accept your offer," he declared, his voice filled with determination.

Abraham Lincoln was reborn, and The Destiny of Tyr bestowed upon him knowledge and power beyond his wildest dreams, preparing him for his mission.

"Now that you have a new life with us, your knowledge and power will increase tenfold," noted Avat'or.

"Still, I would do it all over again. If I had my life to do over again, I would take the long way around, through the meadow, and cross over the forest just to greet the trees and the hummingbirds one more time. I would learn to sit at the feet of those who could lift me up and move from those who sought to hurt me. I would eat more cakes and fewer beans. I would drink much more tea and put my feet on the table. I would eat an extra bowl of stew and buy bigger trousers. I would listen to the sound of music, but I would hearken to the cry of the needy. If I had my life to do over again," Lincoln contemplated. "I may have left Earth behind," he mused, "but my purpose remains the same: to fight for truth, and the greater good."

To this day, the grave of John Wilkes Booth lies undisturbed and lonely for all eternity. The name of Abraham Lincoln will live for centuries to come.

Artifact Twenty-Two

Abraham's Dream

"War is a cruel mistress; she brings glory and suffering, honor and shame."- Abraham Lincoln.

Date: Dimension of Thor 2245 CE

Abraham Lincoln stood on the deck of the ship Deepwater Watchman, his eyes scanning the faces of the assembled crew. They looked at him with a mixture of awe and respect, knowing that this man, who had once been a world leader, now stood before them as a wise and revered figure.

"My friends," Lincoln began, his voice carrying over the sound of the ocean waves, "we stand on the cusp of a great challenge. The fate of humanity is uncertain. But I believe that we have the power within us to bring about peace."

The crew listened intently as Lincoln spoke of the horrors of war, of the toll it took on both the body and the spirit. He spoke of the sacrifices that had been made, the lives that had been lost, and the consequences that had reverberated through the ages.

"What is the nature of war?" Lincoln mused, his gaze turning inward. "Is it not born of fear and ignorance? Is it not fueled by pride and greed? We must rise above these base instincts, my friends. We must recognize that true strength lies not in the wielding of a sword, but in the forging of peace."

The crew fell silent, pondering Lincoln's words. They knew that their journey would be fraught with danger, that they would face adversaries who sought to sow chaos and destruction. In that moment, they found solace in the knowledge that they had a leader who believed in the power of goodness and hope.

As the ship sailed on towards its destiny, towards the fabled shores of Tyr where the forces of darkness awaited, Abraham Lincoln stood at the helm, his gaze fixed on the horizon.

"Let us be beacons of hope in a world consumed by darkness," Lincoln declared, his voice ringing out across the deck. "Let us be the ones who bring peace where there is strife, who bring light where there is darkness. For in the end, it is not the might of our swords that will prevail, but the strength of our hearts."

The Deepwater Watchman was surrounded by showers of stars that seemed to whisper forgotten tales of battles long past. The former President found himself in this mysterious place upon a sudden summoning by The Destiny of Tyr.

"President Lincoln," Dragonwülf's voice boomed, resonating with authority and wisdom, "I have called upon you to discuss matters of war and peace, for our worlds are intertwined in ways both seen and unseen. I am in awe of your kind view of peace, but I do not believe that peace can be achieved through diplomats. Evil can only be fought with violent brute force. Evil does not understand the diplomat." Lincoln regarded the warrior with a mix of curiosity and respect. Dragonwülf's piercing eyes met Lincoln's as the president spoke with a gravity that belied his formidable presence.

"On December 26, 1862, thirty-eight Dakota Indians were hanged in Mankato, Minnesota, in the largest mass execution in history. I ordered them hanged. They danced and wailed on top of the gallows, awaiting their execution. Not a day passes that I do not think of them. This is the greatest regret I live with every day. I see their faces in my sleep. I pray that I never forget them, and I pray that God does not permit me to forget them. War is a cruel mistress," said Lincoln. "It brings glory and suffering, honor and shame. In battle, we are tested not only in strength but also in our willingness to lay down our lives for a greater cause. These warriors did nothing more than protect their land. They killed the settlers who tried to steal their homes. Is there anything you would not do to protect you and yours? I still hear their screams."

The two figures began to walk along the deck of the ship, their conversation weaving through the barrels on the deck like a melody of the ages. Lincoln, a man of principles and ideals, sought to understand the complexities of war from a perspective unlike any he had encountered before.

"Tell me, Dragonwülf," Lincoln inquired, "how do the warriors of old reconcile the brutality of war with the ideals of justice and righteousness?"

Dragonwülf paused, his gaze turning inward as if searching for the right words.

"In battle, we must hold fast to our values even as the world around us descends into chaos. Honor, courage, and loyalty are our guiding stars, shining bright even in the darkest of times."

In the twilight hours, as the stars began to twinkle overhead like distant beacons of hope, Lincoln and Dragonwülf reached a clearing bathed in moonlight. There, they paused; the weight of their conversation hung heavy in the air.

Lincoln began, his voice tinged with both sorrow and resolve, "War may be a necessary evil, but we must strive for peace whenever possible. The true mark of a warrior is not in the battles they win, but in the peace they cultivate."

Avat'or approached Lincoln, "Mr. President, we must discuss an imminent threat that looms over the universe: The Defiler. This malevolent being has plagued our world for centuries, corrupting the purest of hearts and spreading chaos wherever he treads.

We must rid our realm of this evil for the last time. So after much deliberation, we reached a unanimous decision - we would seek the guidance of our newest member of Destiny, and that is you, Mr. Lincoln.

"We seek your counsel on a matter of great urgency. The Defiler threatens to bring imbalance to our universe by sowing violence and discord. We implore you to share with us your wisdom and guide us on how to confront and defeat this ancient evil."

Lincoln listened intently, his expression grave yet determined. After a moment of contemplation, he spoke in his deep, resonant voice. "My friends, the paths to victory over such darkness are not easy ones. But remember, in the face of great evil, it is unity, courage, and unwavering resolve that shall light the way."

The council members nodded in understanding, their eyes reflecting determination and hope.

"How do we find this Defiler of Souls?" inquired a valiant warrior, her sword gleaming at her side.

"You must seek out the source of its power, where its malevolence is strongest," Lincoln advised. "Follow the whispers of the wind, the guidance of the stars, and the beating of your own hearts. Trust in each other, and together, you shall uncover his lair."

As Dragonwülf and the Destiny of Tyr ventured forth into the darkness, facing trials and tribulations along the way, they held onto Lincoln's words as a beacon of hope.

Later that night in his quarters, Abraham Lincoln drifted into a dream from his past.

In his dream, Abraham Lincoln sat quietly by the crackling fireplace, the flickering flames casting a warm glow across his weathered face. He glanced up as his young son, Tad, entered the room with a curious expression.

"Father, why do you always seem so wise and always know what to say?" Tad asked.

Lincoln chuckled softly, patting the empty space on the couch beside him.

"Come, sit with me, Tad. I will tell you a story that has been passed down through generations."

As Tad settled in beside his father, Lincoln began to speak in a gentle yet powerful voice.

"In a small village long ago, there lived a wise old man named Samuel. He was known throughout the land for his great wisdom and kind heart." Tad listened intently as his father continued, "There once was a young boy named David who spent his days watching over his father's sheep. While others saw him as just a shepherd, God saw something more. David cared for each sheep. He knew their sounds, their paths, and even risked his life to protect them from lions and bears.

One day, God sent wise Samuel to David's home. Among all of David's strong and tall brothers, God chose David, the smallest and youngest, to one day be king."

"Why would he get chosen if he was so small and just a boy?" asked Tad.

"Man looks at the outward appearance, but the Lord looks at the heart. You see, David did not become king overnight. He still tended sheep, learned patience, and trusted God through quiet days and dark nights. When the time came, David was ready, but not because of his strength, but because of his heart."

Lincoln reached out and ruffled Tad's hair affectionately before replying.

"Wisdom, my son, is not measured by the words we speak or the knowledge we possess. It is reflected in our actions, in how we treat others with kindness and respect, and how we strive to make the world a better place."

As the fire crackled and popped into the silence that followed, Lincoln's words lingered in the air, filling the room with a sense of profound truth and understanding.

"And remember, son," Lincoln concluded, his gaze warm and thoughtful, "wisdom is not a destination to reach, but a journey to embark upon, with an open heart and a willingness to learn from every experience."

The ship rumbled underneath, waking Lincoln from his sweet remembrances and slumber. His heart was warm with memories from the past, but there was much to do, and he was needed to save the world once again.

Artifact Twenty-Three

The Lost Souls of Caligulis Q3

Date: Future Dimension of Thor 2567 CE

Planet Caligulis Q3 in the Galaxy of Lost Souls

"I will not rest until I torture or kill every individual in the galaxy that opposes me. I just want to be loved and worshiped like the old gods. Is that too much to ask?" -The Defiler

The planet Caligulis Q3 hung in the void of space like a desolate wasteland, a penal colony known for housing the most notorious criminals in the universe. The cold, unforgiving surface was scarred with deep crevices and jagged rock formations, illuminated by the eerie glow of the distant stars. On this forsaken world, the Defiler hatched a nefarious plan that threatened to unleash chaos upon the universe.

The Defiler stood atop a towering spire in the heart of the prison compound. His twisted grin revealed a glimpse of his evil intent, plotting his next move.

"We must act quickly," he hissed to his followers, a group of hardened criminals who knelt before him in fear. "The time has come to unleash my fury upon the planets, to bring destruction and chaos to all who oppose us."

Among the gathered criminals was the notorious space serial killer Ogor the spike, a fierce and merciless ghoul with a reputation for plundering entire star systems and leaving their inhabitants impaled at the city gates. His eyes blazed as he listened to the Defiler's words, eager for the chance to wreak havoc once more. Ogor patterned himself after the notorious Vlad the Impaler from Earth's history. His ultimate goal was the same as the Defiler, annihilation and decapitation of the universe.

Meanwhile, far across the galaxy, aboard the ship Deepwater Watchman, Captain Old-Turas stood on the bridge with his loyal crew, his eyes fixed on the space before him. They had learned of the Defiler's sinister plan to release the most dangerous criminals into the universe from Caligulis Q3. This would be a gigantic jump into the panorama of the future.

"We cannot let this happen," Dragonwülf declared, his voice firm with determination. "We must stop the Defiler before it's too late and he floods the universe with evil."

Captain Turas nodded grimly. "We will need to move fast if we are going to prevent a catastrophe of this magnitude. The Defiler will not make it easy for us."

As the Deepwater Watchman hurtled through the vast expanse of space towards Caligulis Q3, the tension on board grew palpable. The crew knew that they were racing against time to thwart the Defiler's plan and prevent the release of the galaxy's most dangerous criminals.

Meanwhile, on the planet, the Defiler spoke to the most heinous criminals, their faces twisted with malice and hunger for chaos. The air was thick with tension as they waited for instructions from their new leader.

The Defiler's voice cut through the silence like a knife. "My loyal followers," he began. "Today, we shall unleash a wave of terror upon the populations of this universe. We shall show them the true extent of our power, and they shall tremble before us. You will be led by Ogor the Spike. You will follow his instructions as you travel the galaxy with me in the Götterdämmerung!"

The criminals before him nodded eagerly, their eyes gleaming with anticipation. They were ready to carry out his every command, no matter how horrible.

"You will go out into the galaxy to kill and destroy wherever you go," The Defiler continued, his eyes blazing with hate. "You will show no mercy, no remorse. Those who stand against us will be crushed beneath our heels."

One of the criminals, a hulking figure whose official Q3 prison number was 101Q3 with jagged scars crisscrossing his face, stepped forward. "What if someone refuses to swear allegiance to you, my Lord?" he growled, his voice rough with hatred.

The Defiler's lips curled into a cruel smile. "Those who refuse to swear their allegiance to me will suffer the most agonizing fate imaginable," he declared, his voice dripping with malice. "They will wish for death. Guards! Seize this piece of excrement and impale him at the front passageway to the ship. He will be a fine example."

"These men with me will not fail me! They do my bidding and will deliver me out of your hands!" 101Q3 threatened. A look of shock and terror covered his face as he realized there was not one man who would move to save him.

"You cowardly snakes! You will pay for this! I will see that each of you is flayed and boiled alive when I escape!" screamed the criminal.

His tortured screams filled the air as the hideous spike was forced upward through his body and out the top of his head, leaving him as a ghoulish example of questioning the Defiler.

The criminals exchanged knowing glances, their eyes filled with a twisted kind of obedience. They were eager to carry out the Defiler's commands, to sow chaos and destruction wherever they went. Most of all, they wanted to be set free to torture the galaxy.

"We will do as you command, my Lord!" The new leader answered.

As the Defiler raised his hand, a dark energy crackled around him, enveloping the criminals in its malevolent embrace. "Now, go forth, my servants!" he commanded, his voice echoing in the desolate landscape. "Show the universe the true power of darkness. Show them that we are the masters of our fate."

The criminals scattered, disappearing into the hull of the Götterdämmerung to carry out the Defilers' wicked bidding. The universe shuddered at the thought of the chaos that was about to be unleashed, as The Defiler watched with a cold, triumphant gleam in his eyes.

Hours passed as the Dragonwülf and The Deepwater approached the prison planet, its surface coming into view through the panorama. The jagged landscape was a grim reminder of the darkness that lurked within, a prison for souls as lost and desolate as the planet itself.

The Deepwater Watchman cut through space like a gleaming blade. The Götterdämmerung and The Defiler were closing in fast. The skies darkened as the two vessels approached each other, a storm brewing overhead as if nature itself sensed the impending clash of titans.

Captain Old-Turas' voice boomed across the decks, rallying his crew for the battle ahead. "Men, prepare yourselves! We face The Defiler and his crew of cutthroats, but do not be afraid, for we are the Watchmen of space and sea!"

The crew of The Deepwater Watchman erupted into cheers, their spirits bolstered by their captain's words. They rushed to their stations, arming themselves with swords, muskets, and cannons, as the Götterdämmerung loomed closer, its black sails billowing ominously in the wind.

As the two ships drew alongside each other, the clash began in earnest. The Defiler, a towering figure clad in tattered black robes, leaped onto the deck of The Deepwater Watchman with a blood-curdling roar to face Dragonwülf in battle. His eyes gleamed with malice as he raised his serrated cutlass, ready to strike down anyone who dared stand in his way.

As Dragonwülf and The Defiler locked eyes, a tense silence fell over the ship, broken only by the sound of clashing steel in the wind. Without a word, they charged at each other, swords clashing in a cacophony of metal strikes.

The Defiler moved with speed and agility, his strikes fierce and unrelenting. Dragonwülf, however, matched him blow for blow, his sword singing through the air.

"Your reign of terror ends here, fiend!" Dragonwülf roared, his voice echoing through the forest.

The Defiler laughed, a chilling sound that sent a shiver down Dragonwülf's spine. "You are a fool to challenge me, Dragonwülf. I am the master of darkness, and your light will be extinguished before me."

Dragonwülf was undaunted, his determination unwavering. With a mighty roar, he unleashed a flurry of strikes, each one aimed at piercing the black heart of his adversary.

The Defiler snarled, his eyes burning with fury as he pushed back against Dragonwülf's assault. The swords clashed and sparked in a dazzling display of skill and valor, the forest echoing with the sounds of their battle.

As the fight raged on, Dragonwülf could feel his strength waning, his blows becoming slower and less precise. With a final, mighty strike, the Defiler disarmed Dragonwülf, sending his sword flying into the abyss of space.

Captain Turas tossed a long saber to Dragonwülf. "I know it is not your sword, my friend, but I am sure it will do!" said the Captain.

Dragonwülf stood proudly, his silver armor gleaming under the pale moonlight.

Suddenly, a crackling energy filled the air as The Defiler, his obsidian armor reflecting the fire burning within him, raised his blood-stained sword and unleashed a deafening roar that shook the very ground beneath them.

"You are a fool and a pitiful old man," the Defiler snarled. "Your pathetic attempts at heroism will be a disaster to you."

Dragonwülf's response was a defiant war cry, his boot heels digging into the scorched earth beneath him as he readied himself for battle. "I will not let you spread your darkness any further," he declared, his voice a thunderous rumble that echoed across the barren landscape.

Dragonwülf and The Defiler engaged in a deadly dance of combat. Each blow landed with a thunderous impact, sending shockwaves rippling through the air as they fought with intensity.

As the battle raged on, Dragonwülf found himself pushed to his limits, the Defiler's relentless assault taking its toll on his noble form. Despite the searing pain that lanced through his body, Dragonwülf refused to yield, drawing upon reserves of strength and courage that he never knew he possessed.

With a mighty roar, Dragonwülf unleashed a devastating flurry of attacks. His saber tore through the Defiler's armor like paper as he drove the dark warrior to his knees.

The Defiler laughed, a sound as chilling as the icy waters below. "You may have courage, but courage alone will not save you from the wrath of space," he taunted, his blade whirling in a deadly dance. The Defiler pushed Dragonwülf through the gates of the ship, forcing him into outer darkness. Dragonwülf's body tumbled repeatedly through space with nothing to stop it from its death tumble.

In the heart of the chaos, Captain Turas faced off against some of the Defiler's crew. Their swords met in a shower of sparks, the clang of steel ringing out across the tumultuous sea. "You may be fearsome, but you face the might of the Deepwater Watchmen now," Turas growled, his eyes blazing with determination.

"I would worry about your leader if I were you..." warned The Defiler as all eyes turned to space. "You can stay and fight, or you can rescue a worthless old warrior. You choose!" said The Defiler.

"Damn you to Hell, you demon!" said the Captain as he and his men retreated to their ship. "Where are those Destiny of Tyr buggers when you need them? Any other time, they would be haunting the deck. Captain Old Turas gazed out of the porthole, his eyes fixed on the drifting figure of Warrior Dragonwülf floating away in the vast expanse of outer space, leaving him stranded and helpless. As he fixed his eyes upon the floating warrior, Old Turas could also see the Götterdämmerung disappear into another corridor of time. The Defiler was gone again.

Hold on! I am coming; you blasted pain in the arse!" Captain Turas shouted as he swiftly prepared to venture out into the cold void of space.

He secured his helmet, and his thoughts raced with concern for his comrade. Turas had known Dragonwülf for years, and their bond on the battlefield was unbreakable. There was no way he would let him drift away into the unknown.

With a determined look on his face, Captain Turas braved the plank and stepped out into the silent emptiness of space. The stars seemed to twinkle knowingly as he propelled himself towards Dragonwülf, whose once proud figure now seemed vulnerable and fragile against the backdrop of distant galaxies.

"Stay calm, I have got you," Turas said, his voice steady and reassuring as he closed the distance between them.

As he reached out to grab Dragonwülf's hand, a sudden tremor shook their surroundings, sending them spinning through space. Turas gritted his teeth, his mind racing to find a solution to their predicament.

"Those slimy cowards are firing upon us! We need to act fast," Turas exclaimed, his voice urgent.

With quick thinking and steady hands, Captain Turas grabbed the guide rope and wrapped it around Dragonwülf's waist.

"Dragonwülf, brace yourself! We're going to make it out of this," Turas said, his determination unwavering despite the odds stacked against them. His crew pulled both men back aboard the ship. The Deepwater Watchman had its Captain back.

The crew tended to their beloved warrior, Dragonwülf. His once fearsome demeanor had been replaced with a look of exhaustion and anger.

As Dragonwülf slowly regained consciousness, the crew gathered around him, their worried expressions showing their concern for their comrade.

"Welcome back. You gave us quite a scare out there," said Viktor Vorobyev."

Dragonwülf's eyes blazed with fury as he struggled to sit up. "I should never have let The Defiler slip through my grasp," he growled, his voice filled with frustration. "He escaped while you were trying to rescue me."

The crew exchanged glances, knowing the gravity of the situation.

"We did everything we could, Dragonwülf," Sir Robert reassured him, his tone firm yet compassionate.

Dragonwülf nodded, his resolve returning despite his weakened state. "I will not rest until we bring him to justice," he declared, and suddenly his eyes filled with determination.

"Óðinn has just told me where the Defiler flees. I do not know why the Allfather talks to me, but I will obey."

The Battle of the Black Vein

The Deepwater Watchman tore through the void like a wounded beast, its hull scorched and bleeding vapor into the stars. Around it, space burned.

A dead moon split open centuries ago hung like a cracked skull nearby, its exposed core vomiting black lightning as the Defiler fed upon it.

On the bridge, red warning sigils screamed.

"Bring the ship Starboard!" Captain Old-Turas roared, blood running down one side of his face. "If that thing hits us again, we're dust!"

The viewscreen flared, and there he was.

The **Defiler** towered in the vacuum, a colossal figure of charred armor and living shadow, wings of writhing void unfurled behind him. Thousands of screaming faces twisted across his armor, forever frozen in agony. In one clawed hand, he held a spear of condensed darkness; in the other, a pulsing knot of stolen souls.

His voice came not through sound—but *inside the mind.*

"Deepwater Watchman… I remember every soul I tore from your decks."

The crew screamed as the lights flickered. Several collapsed, clutching their skulls as blood leaked from their eyes.

"Hold the line!" Old-Turas shouted. "Gunners.FIRE!"

Cannons thundered. Lances of white-hot energy slammed into the Defiler, exploding against his armor.

He laughed and hurled the spear.

It punched through the Watchman's starboard side, shredding metal and bodies alike. Three crewmen were atomized instantly—another was torn in half, his upper torso floating away, entrails boiling into vapor.

"The engine room is cooked!" someone screamed.

Then a new light split the void. A *roar,* ancient and divine.

Morning Fire of the Sky burst from hyperspace in a cyclone of flame, her wings spanning kilometers, her scales burning gold and crimson. Astride her back stood Dragonwulf, armor glowing with runes of Tyr, his great blade already drawn.

"Defiler!" Dragonwulf thundered. "You had forgotten I knew where you were hiding."

Morning Fire exhaled a blaze of fire.

Dragonflame slammed into the Defiler, engulfing him completely. Space itself screamed as fire consumed stolen souls by the thousands. Faces melted from his armor, shrieking as they were *freed*.

The Defiler staggered back for the first time in an age.

"You have learned new things! How were you to know I was still in possession of countless souls?" asked the Defiler.

"Let us just say our Gods will not be mocked, shall we?"

Dragonwulf leapt and crossed the distance in a heartbeat, landing on the Defiler's chest with enough force to crack moons. His blade came down, cleaving through shadow-armor, carving a glowing wound straight through the Defiler's torso.

Black blood thick with screaming spirits erupted from his gored chest cavity.

The Defiler howled in eternal pain.

Morning Fire slammed into him next, jaws closing around one wing. She *ripped*, tearing void-flesh and bone free, flinging the severed limb spinning into space.

The Defiler struck back.

A blast of soul-energy exploded outward, slamming Dragonwulf into an asteroid hard enough to shatter it. His armor cracked; blood floated from his mouth in ruby spheres.

Morning Fire screamed in fury and pain as chains of darkness wrapped around her neck and wings, digging in, burning.

"I will wear your dragon's screams as a crown!" the Defiler roared.

Dragonwulf pushed himself up, snarling, eyes blazing.

"No," he growled. "You will *run*."

He raised his blade and spoke the ancient command of Tyr.

The sword ignited—white, gold, and blue—pure destiny given edge.

Dragonwulf charged again, hacking relentlessly. Each blow tore chunks of the Defiler apart—arms severed, armor shattered, souls bursting free in blinding flashes. Morning Fire broke the chains and unleashed claw and flame, raking the Defiler until his massive form was reduced to a torn, leaking ruin.

The Defiler staggered, barely holding himself together.

For the first time—

He was afraid.

"This is not the end," he hissed, his form unraveling into shadow. "I will return. I always do."

Dragonwulf hurled his blade.

It pierced the Defiler's skull, pinning him to the corpse of the dead moon.

The Defiler screamed—then *vanished*, dissolving into a vortex of darkness that tore open reality itself before snapping shut.

Silence fell.

The Deepwater Watchman drifted, broken but alive.

On the bridge, Old-Turas exhaled shakily. "Tell me… please… that bastard's dead."

Dragonwulf floated back toward Morning Fire, retrieving his blade as he mounted her once more.

"No," he said grimly. "I do not know what it will take to kill him, but he bleeds. And now he knows fear. *He bleeds*.

Morning Fire growled, embers smoldering between her teeth.

The war was far from over.

And the galaxy had just felt it awaken.

The Shattering of the Veiled Throne

The Defiler of Souls did not flee from the battle.

He fled deeper.

Reality peeled back like torn flesh as he forced himself through the Veil Between Heavens, dragging his ruined essence into a forbidden dominion older than gods. His body reformed slowly—wrongly—bones knitting backward, shadows screaming as they fused.

He collapsed upon the *Veiled Throne, a massive structure grown from petrified angels and extinct stars.*

He was bleeding fear.

"Dragonwulf…" he rasped, clutching the hole where a heart should have been. " Y*ou are Warden of Tyr*. I should have known that!"

Around him, some ancient spirits stirred. They wereancient entities chained in orbit, their forms half-thought, half-nightmare.

One spoke, its voice like grinding galaxies.

"You were nearly unmade."

The Defiler snarled, ripping a soul from the air and devouring it whole. The scream echoed forever.

"Nearly," he hissed. "Means *alive*."

He rose, his armor reforming in jagged fragments.

"If the Warden walks the stars… then the stars will scream his name as they die."

Dragonwulf did not celebrate. He stood alone upon the fractured hull of the Deepwater Watchman, Morning Fire of the Sky coiled protectively around him, her wounds steaming. Dragonwulf stiffened. His blade hummed low and urgent.

Morning Fire lifted her head, eyes narrowing. "He is not done," she growled.

Before Dragonwulf could answer, the sky split open, revealing the sea below.

The Phantom of the Sea emerged half memory, half storm, draped in spectral chains and ancient oaths. His voice rolled like waves breaking against doomed shores.

"Warden of Tyr," the Phantom intoned. "The Defiler has broken the Final Seal."

Dragonwulf clenched his fist. " Who? Where?"

The Phantom gestured, and the universe screamed.

A distant system imploded in slow agony. Entire worlds were being *harvested,* their souls pulled into a spiraling cathedral of darkness.

The Phantom continued:

"The Defiler prepares the Ascension Rite. When complete… he will no longer flee."

Morning Fire snarled, flames leaking from her jaws. "Then we burn him before it ends."

The Phantom turned his hollow gaze to Dragonwulf.

"You will not face this alone."

With a thunderclap, the heavens opened.

Ships, ancient, resurrected, impossible, poured forth. Warrior-kings long dead. Sorcerers bound by oath. The fallen crew of battles past, reborn in spectral armor.

A voice echoed from every direction. Countless voices united as one.

"Warden of Tyr. Command us."

Dragonwulf stepped forward.

He raised his blade. The runes ignited so brightly that even stars dimmed in respect. "Then hear me," he said, voice calm, lethal. "The Defiler has chosen extinction."

He pointed toward the collapsing system.

"We bring war."

Morning Fire unfurled her wings, roaring—a sound that shattered moons in distant orbits.

The Veiled Throne Armada surged forward.

And somewhere, upon the Veiled Throne, the Defiler of Souls *smiled* because the next battle would not be an ambush.

It would be the end of an age.

Ogor the Impaler

Dragonwülf sat still on the edge of his bunk after a long sleep when he was greeted by Old-Turas.

"Are you not going to thank me for saving your worthless pelt?" asked the Captain.

"I will just owe you yet another one," he answered tongue-in-cheek. The room grew silent with a long, awkward pause in their conversation.

"So do I have to guess what is on your mind? We are in pursuit of the Defiler. He cannot hide forever," said Old Turas with hope in his voice.

"We must stop him before he kills again. We came so close."

"What else worries you?" I know there is something else. Am I right?" asked a curious Old Turas.

"Yes, I am afraid of something I thought was gone long ago."

"Well, spit it out, you old fool, what is it?"

"Not what but who," added Dragonwülf. He is someone from my past battles, *Ogor the Impaler*. Of all the enemies, demons, and ghouls I have battled in the past, he is far worse than the worst of them. I left him for dead on the battlefield many years ago. He had a she-wolf for a companion, and I fought the devil dog for hours until I vanquished her, but not before she sank a claw into my face. I was distracted by Ogor and his minions and lost my edge in battle."

"That is why you carry that Wolf-claw in your face?" asked a bewildered Old Turas. "I never knew the story."

"I keep it there to remind me of focus in battle and in all things. I even adopted it as my nickname," said the old warrior.

"The battlefield where we met was a graveyard of smoke and broken banners," recounted Dragonwülf. "Iron stakes jutted from the frozen ground like the teeth of a god long dead, and upon each one hung the still forms of men, soldiers of Arom, their armor painted in the crimson paint of death.

Then I beheld the ultimate evil. It was the figure of Ogor, clad in plates of blackened chain-mail and his helmet shaped like the skull of a wolf. In his gauntlet, he held a spear so long it bent under its own weight, its point slick with the blood of the condemned. To his side was For'Mir, the she-wolf. She stood nearly to his chest in staggering height.

He turned as a young soldier stumbled into the clearing, wide-eyed and trembling."

'You did this,' the soldier whispered, voice breaking. 'You monster…'

"Ogor's reply was calm, deep, and almost reverent."

'Monster?' he tilted his head, as if considering. 'No, boy. I am the consequence.'

"The soldier's courage flared for a moment."

'You serve the Demons! You are the one who devours the dead!'

"A low laugh came from within Ogor's helmet like stones grinding together in a low, menacing rumble."

'For'Mir has tasted of man flesh today. He has greased his chin with the lifeblood of the brave,' he hissed.

"Stand fast and deliver yourself unto me, you ghoul of the devil. I will hear no more of this. Pray to whatever god, devil, or idol you pray because your corpse is mine today. Tell me who you serve," I demanded. "I could not stand by and watch this happen."

'I serve what remains when gods forget mercy. The Defiler of Souls shows me the truth. The truth is that souls are but echoes, and echoes fade unless chained to pain.'

"He stepped closer, boots crunching over the frozen earth."

'Do you know why they call me the Impaler?'

"I shook my head," trembling. "I can imagine why."

'I learned that pain speaks to the world,' Ogor said. 'The dying people suffer and weep, and the world remembers.'

"You do not strike fear in me today," I said. "You will pay for this massacre with your own blood," I said as I drew my long sword and held it before me. "The rain fell in black sheets across the ruins of Esgarth. Lightning flared over the broken spires. In the name of the old and new Gods, I command you to die at my blade," I bellowed.

'Your useless Gods cannot save you,' Ogor hissed, his voice carrying as iron dragged over stone. 'I have bathed in the blood of Kings and crushed their bones beneath my boots. You will join both the Gods and Kings in the dirt.'

The first clash was like thunder. The wolf and Ogor attacked. The fang met the Spear in a storm of sparks. Dragonwülf twisted, parrying Ogor's downward thrust, the runes of his sword shrieking against the infernal edge. Ogor drove forward, his strength monstrous, forcing me back through the mud.

The wolf lunged too fast to see—and her fangs tore across my face, drawing blood that shimmered like liquid fire. I staggered, clutching the wound.

Her fang had broken off and was lodged in my face. The old warrior swung his broad sword over the head of the she-wolf, separating her from her head right above the shoulders. Ogor shrieked from within his filthy spirit. He emitted a mournful, angry groan that could be heard throughout the Esgarth Mountains.

The final clash split the night. My sword met Ogor's spear once more, then shattered it. My sword drove through Ogor's chest, pinning him to the earth. He screamed, not a human sound, but a thousand damned voices tearing loose at once. His armor melted, his flesh turned to ash, and the wind carried him away like smoke."

"Why have you not told me of this before? Over the many sea voyages and battles we were in together, you never mentioned Ogor the Impaler. "I think I would have remembered that," said Old –Turas as he listened to the tale.

"I believed I had left him for dead. There was no reason to let his name live on," explained Dragonwülf. "In our battle with the Defiler, I am certain I saw the very face of the Impaler directly to his right hand. He has returned to the feet of the Defiler. I do not know how or why, but it is true. I saw him as certain as I see you. Before he became the right hand of the Defiler, Ogor was a knight of Hrothgorn sworn to protect the border fortresses along the Mountains of Esgarth. In those days, he was called Ogor the Faithful, a man of iron honor and unbreakable loyalty. When the Armada of the Dead rose from the Undersea of Morak, his garrison was the first to fall. His men were drowned, resurrected, and turned against him. He prayed to the gods for deliverance, and none came, and the only god that answered was the Defiler. In the black of the night, when his fortress burned and his sword arm failed, Ogor heard a voice whisper through the flames."

'Serve me, Ogor of Hrothgorn, and I shall grant you what your gods have denied you, victory, and remembrance.'

"Ogor, broken and betrayed, accepted. The next dawn, his heart hollowed by shadow and his veins filled with the Defiler's curse. He slaughtered the invaders, and then his own surviving soldiers impaled them upon the walls of his keep so their screams would echo across the valley. They say the Defiler appeared to him in that moment, in a shape of mist and bone," recounted the old warrior from the corridors of his memory.

'Prepare the world for my awakening,' the Defiler hissed. 'Impale it upon its own sins.'

After a long silence, Old-Turas spoke.

"Should we tell the others about the Impaler?"

"Yes, we will, but let us wait until the right time, "said Dragonwulf. "It will be soon enough."

The Deepwater Watchman continues through the Panorama of time.

Acknowledgments

FRIENDS OF DRAKWNÚLFR

Kára María Fagr (Kára Marie the Fair). Karen Marie DeBella (Lady Dragonwülf)

Dragon's Den Books, Arcadia, Florida

Barnes & Noble, 71st Street, Tulsa.

Tulsa Technology Center Riverside Campus/ Kim Streater

Joe Bouchard

The music of Blue Öyster Cult

Rob Halford and the music of Judas Priest/ Invincible Shield

The music of Antti Martikainen

The Estate of JRR Tolkien

Rivendell Books in Broken Arrow, OK.

Astrid and Eric Pensa

Two Steps from Hell & the Epic Music of Thomas Bergersen

Dean and Martha Oglesby

Dr. Paul Cochran

Doug and Christie Friend

Floor Jansen and Nightwish

Salvatore' DeBella

And of course,
Professor John Ronald Reuel Tolkien

Illustrations courtesy of CANVA

Salvatore DeBella is the author of the *Dragonwulf* saga, an epic fantasy series blending Norse mythology, cosmic warfare, and brutal heroism. Drawing inspiration from classic sword-and-sorcery authors such as R.A. Salvatore, DeBella crafts worlds where gods bleed, dragons burn the heavens, and destiny is both a curse and a calling.

His debut novel, *Dragonwulf Book I: The Destiny of Tyr*, was published in December 2023, followed by *Dragonwulf Book II: Twilight of the Gods* and the third volume of the series in 2025, *Dragonwulf Book III: The Age of Metal*. The series has become known for its relentless action, dark mythological themes, and cinematic scope that stretches from ancient battlefields to the farthest reaches of the cosmos.

When he is not forging legends and shattering pantheons, DeBella lives in Glenpool, Oklahoma, where he continues to expand the *Dragonwulf* universe and explore new tales of fallen gods, eternal warriors, and the fragile balance of creation.

Next in the Series Book III: *The Age of Metal and*

Dragonwulf Book IV: The Shattered Heavens

Salvatore DeBella, often known as "Sal," is an American author and public speaker specializing in epic fantasy and science fiction with a modern twist.

Literary Work:

He is best known for the Dragonwülf series, which he describes as a "cinematic fusion" of Norse mythology and futuristic elements. The trilogy includes:

(2022): His debut novel centers on an ancient civilization discovered in the 19th century and an ancient warrior named Wolfclaw.

(2024) Dragonwülf Book II: Twilight of the Gods Continues the saga of rising warriors and falling gods.

(2025)Dragonwülf Book III: The Age of Metal

To be released in 2026, Dragonwülf Book IV: The Shattered Heavens

Style and Influences

Writing Philosophy: DeBella aims for an immersive, movie-like reading experience. He often uses the term "Interdimensional Synchrony" to describe his blend of genres.

Influences: His work is heavily influenced by Edgar Allan Poe, J.R.R. Tolkien, the progressive rock band Blue Öyster Cult, and fantasy legend R.A. Salvatore.

Background and Personal Life

Education and Career: Born in Pittsfield, Massachusetts, he holds a Bachelor
of Arts in English Education with an emphasis in English Literature
from Northeastern State University. He spent his career as a college instructor
before turning to writing in 2015.

Residency: He currently lives in Glenpool, Oklahoma, with his wife, Karen.

Salvatore' DeBella

Author Page (E-mail, etc.)

saldebella@gmail.com

Webpage
https://saldebella.wixsite.com/website

Facebook Page
https://www.facebook.com/sal.debella.7

X

https://twitter.com/sal_debella